BOOK

Brother in the Land

Robert Swindells left school at the age of fifteen and joined the Royal Air Force at seventeen-and-a-half. After his discharge, he worked at a variety of jobs, before training and working as a teacher. He is now a full-time writer and lives with his wife Brenda on the Yorkshire Moors. Robert Swindells has written many books for young people, and in 1984 was the winner of the Children's Book Award and the Other Award for his novel *Brother in the Land*. He won the Children's Book Award for a second time in 1990 with *Room 13*, and in 1994 *Stone Cold* won the Carnegie Medal and the Sheffield Children's Book Award.

This edition has a new final chapter.

Robert Swindells

Brother in
the Land

PUFFIN BOOKS
in association with Oxford University Press

PUFFIN BOOKS

Published by the Penguin Group
Penguin Books Ltd, 27 Wrights Lane, London W8 5TZ, England
Penguin Putnam Inc., 375 Hudson Street, New York, New York 10014, USA
Penguin Books Australia Ltd, Ringwood, Victoria, Australia
Penguin Books Canada Ltd, 10 Alcorn Avenue, Toronto, Ontario, Canada M4V 3B2
Penguin Books (NZ) Ltd, Private Bag 102902, NSMC, Auckland, New Zealand

On the World Wide Web at: www.penguin.com

Penguin Books Ltd, Registered Offices: Harmondsworth, Middlesex, England

First published by Oxford University Press 1984
Published in Puffin Books 1985
Reprinted in Penguin Books 1988
Reissued in Puffin Books 1994
10

Filmset in Sabon

Made and printed in England by Clays Ltd, St Ives plc

British Library Cataloguing in Publication Data
A CIP catalogue record for this book is available from the British Library

ISBN 0–140–37300–4

'He who places his brother in the land is everywhere.'
The Papyrus Ipuwer.

BEFORE

East is East and West is West, and maybe it was a difference of opinion or just a computer malfunction. Either way, it set off a chain of events that nobody but a madman could have wanted and which nobody, not even the madmen, could stop.

There were missiles.
Under the earth.
In the sky.
Beneath the waves.
Missiles with thermo-nuclear warheads, enough to kill everybody on earth.
Three times over.

And something set them off; sent them flying, West to East and East to West, crossing in the middle like cars on a cable-railway.

East and West, the sirens wailed. Emergency procedures began, hampered here and there by understandable panic. Helpful leaflets were distributed and roads sealed off. VIPs went to their bunkers and volunteers stood at their posts. Suddenly, nobody wanted to be an engine-driver anymore, or a model or a rock-star. Everybody wanted to be one thing: a survivor. But it was an overcrowded profession.

The missiles climbed their trajectory arcs, rolled over the top and came down, accelerating. Below, everyone was ready. The Frimleys had their shelter in the lounge. The Bukovskys favoured the cellar. A quick survey would have revealed no overwhelming preference, worldwide, for one part of the house over the others.

Down came the missiles. Some had just the one warhead, others had several, ranging from the compact, almost tactical warhead to the large, family size. Every town was to receive its own, individually-programmed warhead. Not one had been left out.

They struck, screaming in with pinpoint accuracy, bursting with blinding flashes, brighter than a thousand suns. Whole towns and city-centres vaporized instantly; while tarmac, trees and houses thirty miles from the explosions burst into flames. Fireballs, expanding in a second to several miles across, melted and devoured all matter that fell within their diameters. Blast-waves, travelling faster than sound, ripped through the suburbs. Houses disintegrated and vanished. So fierce were the flames that they devoured all the oxygen around them, suffocating those people who had sought refuge in deep shelters. Winds of a hundred-and-fifty miles an hour, rushing in to fill the vacuum, created fire-storms that howled through the streets, where temperatures in the thousands cooked the subterranean dead. The very earth heaved and shook as the warheads rained down, burst upon burst upon burst, and a terrible thunder rent the skies.

For an hour the warheads fell, then ceased. A great silence descended over the land. The Bukovskys had gone, and the Frimleys were no more. Through the silence, through the pall of smoke and dust that blackened the sky, trillions of deadly radioactive particles began to fall. They fell soundlessly, settling like an invisible snow on the devastated earth.

Incredibly, here and there, people had survived the bombardment. They lay stunned in the ruins, incapable of thought. Drifting on the wind, the particles sifted in upon them, landing unseen on clothing, skin and hair, so that most of these too would die, but slowly.

Most, but not all. There were those whose fate it was to wander this landscape of poisonous desolation. One of them was me.

ONE

It was a hot day in the summer holidays. People kept coming in the shop for ice-cream and lollies and coke. We lived in Skipley, behind the shop, open seven days a week and the bell drove you daft. I'd have gone off on the bike but Mum said I had to play with Ben.

You know what it's like playing with a kid of seven. They always want to play at being in the army or something. They get so wrapped up being a soldier that they yell stupid stuff at the tops of their voices so the grownups can hear. It's embarrassing.

Anyway, I played with him a bit in the back where Dad stacked the crates. It was all right at first but then he started wittering; so when Dad went off in the van, I gave him ten pence for a lolly. He ran inside and I got on the bike and left.

It didn't matter where I went, so long as I got away by myself. I had thought of going into Branford but there were too many people there, so I took the road that goes up over the moor. It's a hard pull and I was sweating like a pig when it flattened out. There's nothing to stop the sun up there and it beat down so you could hear it. The heat made the horizon shimmer and the road look wet. I kept pedalling till I was well away from Skipley, then got off and lay on my back in the needle-grass and looked for UFOs.

It was so quiet you could hear bees in the heather sounding

like a sawmill a long way off. The air smelt of peat and hot tar. The sweat on my shirt made my back cold while the sun burnt my knees through my jeans. Now and then a car went by. It sounds kind of sad now, bees and cars and heather, but that's how it was then.

I must have dozed off, because the next thing I knew the sun was gone and half the sky had vanished behind these great black clouds. It was still hot, but with a different sort of heat; that close, threatening heat you get before a storm.

I didn't fancy being caught out here in a storm. They say lightning strikes the highest point, and there were no trees on the moor. As soon as I stood up, I'd be the highest point. I got up, grabbed the bike and began pedalling like mad towards home.

I nearly made it. The top of the last upward bit was in sight when there came a rumbling in the distance and the first big raindrops fell. Pennies from Heaven, my mum called them.

I might easily have gone on. I had only to top that little slope and I'd have free-wheeled all the way down into Skipley, and I'd have been dead, like everybody else. The reason I didn't was because I spotted the pillbox.

It was one of those concrete bunkers left over from the war, World War Two, not the last one. It was just beyond the ditch, on the edge of farmland, partly sunk into the ground and half-hidden in a clump of elder bushes.

I'd been in it before, years back when Dad brought Mum and me and Ben up for a picnic one day when Ben was a baby. I'd gone crouching into the musty dimness, half expecting to find a machine-gun or a skeleton or something. There'd been an empty bottle and the remains of a fire, and I'd played at shooting up passing cars through the narrow slot.

I couldn't crouch into it now. It had sunk a bit deeper and I was a lot taller and I had to get down on my hands and knees. I lugged the bike across the ditch, propped it against the pillbox and crawled in. The remains of the fire were still there, or perhaps it was another one. I didn't go right in, just far enough so I could watch the storm without getting wet. I used to like thunderstorms as long as I was somewhere safe.

As I crawled in there was this sudden gust of wind and a clap of thunder, and the rain really started coming down. It fell so hard you could feel the ground trembling under you. It poured off the top of the pillbox in a solid curtain. I sat looking out through it, hugging my knees and thinking how smart I'd been to get myself under cover.

Then I saw the flash. It was terrifically bright. I screwed up my eyes and jerked my head away. I thought the bunker had been struck: I expected the whole thing to split apart and fall on top of me.

Then the ground started shaking. It quivered so strongly and so fast that it was like sitting with your eyes closed in an express train. Bits started falling on my head; dust and that. I was choking. I rolled over and lay on my side with my arms wrapped round my head.

There was this sudden hot blast. It drove rain in through the doorway and spattered it on my arms and neck; warm rain. I opened my eyes. The pillbox was flooded with bright, dusty light which flickered and began to fade as I watched. My ear was pressed to the ground and I could hear rumbling way down, like dragons in a cave; receding, growing more faint as the dragons went deeper, till you couldn't hear them at all. The light dimmed and there was only silence, and a pinkish glow with dust in it.

Sometimes, I wish I'd stayed there. The dust would have covered me and I would have slipped away, to follow the dragons down into silence. There are worse things than dragons. I've seen them.

TWO

I lay there for a long time. The freak storm had passed over but it was still raining and I heard thunder now and then in the distance. The atmosphere was still oppressive and I wondered whether it might return, as storms sometimes do.

Presently though, the distant sounds ceased. I didn't fancy riding home in the rain but it showed no sign of easing off, so I sat up. My clothes were covered with dust and my head itched. I made a half-hearted attempt to knock some of it off, then crawled to the doorway.

It was then I saw the cloud, perched like an obscene mushroom on its crooked stem, and the glow from Branford. An icy flood from my guts went up my back and spread across my scalp. I knelt, moving my head slowly from side to side as my brain rejected what my eyes were seeing.

Beyond the near horizon lay a pulsating arc of orange light. It breathed in and out like a living thing, its glow reflected on the bellies of the clouds. It was twilight, and the pall of smoke made a darker stain against the grey.

A teacher brought this book to school once, Protect and Survive or some such title. It reckoned to tell what would happen if H-bombs fell on Britain. It was pretty horrible, but it didn't tell the half of it. Not the half. It had a lot in it: the burns and the blast and the radiation and all. But there was nothing about not knowing what's happened to you; how it leaves you useless, so that you sit staring at the ground instead of looking for food or building a shelter or something. It had bits in about helping one another, only you don't do that. Not for a long time. Other people are shadows that pass you by, or enemies after your stuff. They didn't know that. None of us did. If we had, we wouldn't have done it.

Anyway, when I saw that cloud I knew what it was. I'd seen enough pictures and read enough articles. The papers and TV had been full of stuff about deteriorating relations and red-alerts and all that, only I hadn't taken much interest. It seemed to have been like that on and off, ever since I could remember. I mean, you get used to things and they roll off you. I don't recall anybody being particularly worried round our way. One minute everything was normal, and then it was gone.

I didn't know then what had happened in Skipley. Skipley's five miles from Branford and I could see that no bomb had dropped on it. I guess I thought everybody in Skipley would be okay, as I was myself, until the fallout came that is, I knew there'd be deaths then all right. I'd read about it. That's why I decided to stay in the pillbox. If I'd looked a bit more carefully I might have seen the smoke, but I didn't. I was half-daft with the shock, I suppose. I crawled right to the back of the pillbox and curled up in a corner among the tins and bottles and bits of paper and lay there, pretending everything was all right, till the screaming started.

THREE

It was dark when I heard it. I'd been asleep: God knows how. I guess it was my mind's way of denying reality. Anyway, I woke up suddenly and there was this awful noise; a sort of moaning, and a shuffling sound outside the bunker. I lay rigid, biting my lip, something was moving about out there, something big. I heard the rattle and scrape of branches and something heavy fell to the ground. I felt the impact and dug my nails into my palms, willing the thing to go away; willing it not to find the doorway. A low moan subsided into a wet, bubbly sound that went on and on.

I couldn't move. Something hideous was lying out there in the darkness; its face, if it had one, inches from my own. The hiss of its breath penetrated the concrete and I imagined I could smell it.

I lay, damply terrified, breathing quietly through my mouth. My eyes were open. Shoals of phantom lights floated across the blackness that pressed down on them. And as I lay listening I heard other sounds, fainter and farther away. Out there in the darkness people were screaming.

I saw a film once about Pompeii: people blundering through murky streets as the ash came down. It sounded like that.

Presently, I became aware that the thing outside had gone quiet. I listened intently but there was nothing, only the Pompeiian voices far off. Perhaps it's holding its breath, I thought, listening for me. I held myself soundless for some time but the breathing never resumed and I told myself the thing had moved off. I felt my way to the doorway and peered out.

The glow from Branford had shrunk to a thin flush but now, against the backdrop of night, I saw that Skipley was burning. The rain had stopped and a cool breeze from the moor seemed to clear my mind. I felt a rush of what I can only call normal emotion.

My family. Mum and Dad and Ben. Here I was, skulking in my bunker while God knew what had become of them. They might be dead. Maybe some of the cries I had heard were theirs.

Stricken with fright and guilt, I scrambled from the pillbox and stood up. The bike had fallen over. I picked it up and began shoving it towards the ditch. I must get home; find them. We could go away; take the van and drive north to the lakes and mountains before the fallout got us.

The fallout. As I reached the ditch it started to drizzle and something I'd read; a phrase, flashed across my mind. Black rain. After they dropped the bomb on Hiroshima it rained, and the rain brought down all the radioactive dust from the atmosphere. Thousands of people from the outskirts of the city, who'd survived the actual explosion, got rained on by this stuff and died of radiation-sickness. Afterwards, the scientists called it black rain, because it ended up killing nearly as many people as the bomb itself.

I guess I panicked. It wasn't the cold drops hitting my face, so much as the name. Black rain. It was like something filthy was falling on me out of the sky and I couldn't even see it. Anyway, I dropped the bike and ran back doubled up trying to shield my head with my arms, as if that would do any good. Inside the bunker I used the front of my tee-shirt to scrub the stuff off my hair, face and neck. My arms were spattered too, so I tore the garment off and wiped them with it. Then I screwed it up and shoved it out through the slot. I was crazy.

After that I sat propped up in a corner with my bare back to the concrete. It was fantastically cold. I crossed my arms on my chest and held onto my shoulders and sat there waiting to get

11

sick. I had a fantasy that I'd die like this and that someday, centuries from now maybe, somebody would find my skeleton, still hugging itself trying to get warm.

Outside, the noises never stopped. Voices, and a bang now and then, like something exploding down in the town. Sometimes a voice would come quite close, but mostly they were far away. I know it sounds rotten but I tried not to hear. The rain was falling on them and there was nothing I could do.

I dozed a bit eventually, and came to with a start to find daylight filtering through the slot. Rain was hissing onto the concrete and a line of bright droplets hung from its upper lip, falling now and then in random sequence. I sat half-paralysed with cold, watching them, trying to see the deadly motes inside. Apart from the rain it was quiet now.

I was thirsty. I was hungry too, but it was the thirst that bothered me most. I was struck by the irony of the situation. Outside, the ground was sodden. Pools were forming in every hollow and the ditch was filling up. The clouds, the earth, and the air between were laden with water yet none of it was any use to me.

I remembered that poem about the Ancient Mariner, dying of thirst with an ocean all round him. Water, water everywhere, nor any drop to drink: something like that. It kept going round and round in my head as I watched the bright drips falling across the slot.

It was that which first made me understand the enormity of what had happened. Nuclear missiles had fallen on England, and if they'd fallen on England they must have fallen on a lot of other countries too. This rain, black rain, was falling now on each of them; falling into rivers and reservoirs, tanks and troughs; drifting down on sheep and cows and crops; seeping through the soil to contaminate wells and subterranean lakes.

Water, water everywhere, nor any drop to drink.

I had not felt ill on waking and, I suppose, had entertained subconscious thoughts of long-term survival. Now, with a parched throat and a tongue like a warm slug in my mouth, I thrust such notions aside. Everything needs water. A person can only live a few days without it. Now all the water was contaminated. Whatever survivors there might be would bring about their own deaths as soon as they drank.

I wondered what it felt like to die of thirst. It hurt already, and the process had scarcely begun. Nevertheless, I felt I could never bring myself to drink black rain. It would be the same as swallowing poison. I'd read some stuff about radiation sickness and it sounded horrible. Dying of thirst couldn't possibly be as bad as that. I spent some time massaging a bit of warmth into my limbs, then lay down on my side to await the end.

FOUR

As I said before, sometimes I wish I'd stayed there, but I didn't. I lay all that day and all night too. I got hungrier, thirstier and colder, but no nearer to death so far as I could tell. I slept, on and off. In the end I started thinking about my family again; whether they might be alive and if they were looking for me. I got to wishing I hadn't thrown my shirt away, and I remembered that there was a bar of chocolate in my saddle-bag. I couldn't hear any rain, and with dawn a phantom in the slot, I got up.

I sat for a while, rubbing my arms and chest. My legs felt like New Zealand mutton and a monkey had slept in my mouth. I felt lousy, and wondered if this was the start of the sickness. After a while I felt better and crawled to the doorway, stiff as a board.

I didn't see much at first. Everything seemed normal. It crossed my mind that maybe I'd dreamed it all. I hadn't.

I crawled right out and stood up. A light mist hung on the still air and a glow lit the sky to the east. I started to walk round the pillbox. Water from the drenched grass struck cold through my trainers. I rounded an angle, and cried out.

He lay on his back with his mouth open. One side of his face was a mass of raw flesh. Great, puffy blisters clustered round the eye, reducing it to a slit. His elbows rested on the ground and his forearms stood vertical, the hands hanging like wilted flowers over his chest.

I had almost walked into the raw, hairless scalp. Appalled, I backed off and stood, unable to tear my eyes away.

My first corpse: the first of many. A few weeks later I would scarcely have spared it a glance, except to note that it wore a pair of strong shoes, and to take them. For the moment, though, I stared. Without wanting to, I took in every detail of this thing that had been a man; this thing from whose mouth unhuman sounds had issued as it gasped out its life in the rain: the charred, sodden jacket; the seared flesh; the single, sightless eye.

I felt like puking, but I didn't. The first glimpse had driven into my mouth that flood of sour fluid that precedes vomiting, but instead of spitting it out I had swallowed it, easing the pain in my throat. I didn't know it then, but that's what corpses would mean to me in future; the chance to get something for nothing. A coat perhaps, or a pair of shoes. Something to ease the pain.

I don't know how long I stood there, or what it was that made me move on. It might have been the chocolate, because I remember finding that and squatting by the ditch, shoving it into my mouth. Or it could have been the cold, because I found my shirt under the slot and put it on, wet as it was. Anyway, by the time I'd eaten the chocolate I'd decided what to do.

I'd decided I might as well forget about the black rain for a kick-off. It was everywhere, including the insides of my shoes, so whatever I did now; even if I crawled right back in the bunker, I had irradiated feet. If I was going to die of radiation-sickness, then that was the way it had to be. In the meantime, I'd bike it down into town and see if I could find my family.

The chocolate had warmed me up a bit and the sun was rising. I suppose it was about five a.m. I pulled the bike out of the ditch, wiped the saddle with my shirt and began pedalling slowly up the slope, sick with apprehension as to what I'd see from the top. As it turned out, there was to be a bit more fun for me before I found out.

FIVE

There was this track halfway up the slope, that led off to Kershaw Farm. Nobody ever used it: Old Man Kershaw was a recluse with a big dog.

I was passing the end of the track when I heard a motor. A Land-Rover appeared over the ridge and came racing down the track. You couldn't see the farm from the road because it lay beyond this ridge.

With a surge of thankfulness that I'd found at least one survivor like myself, I braked and waited. The vehicle bounced down the ruts and screeched to a stop where the track joined the road.

I suppose I'd expected Old Man Kershaw. What I got was like something out of a movie. The nearside door opened and this thing jumped out. It was some sort of black, one-piece suit with a face mask, and carried a gun. I could see another one watching me through the windscreen. The one with the gun trotted over.

'Where have you come from?' He was speaking through a mike or something and his tone was harsh. I nodded up the road.

'Skipley. I'm off there now.' The gun made me nervous.

'What were you doing out here?'

I shrugged. 'Hiding. I was in the pillbox when –'

'You're not allowed out here. This road's an ESR. Civilians

must remain where they are.'

I searched the mask for eyes, but the eyepieces were reflective. I said, 'Are you some kind of warden or something; can you tell me what's happening?'

A tinny, quacking sound issued from the mike; the travesty of a laugh. He shifted the gun on its sling. 'I'm not here to answer questions. Leave the bike and get back to town or be shot for looting.'

'Looting?' I showed him my empty hands. 'What d'you mean, leave the bike? It's mine!'

He moved so fast I hadn't time to think. He lifted his leg, planted the sole of his boot on my thigh and pushed. I went sprawling on the asphalt with the bike across my legs. He bent, snatched up the bike and threw it behind him.

'Now get up and get out.' He stood over me with his legs apart and the gun on his hip like Clint Eastwood or somebody. You could tell he liked himself.

I should have done what he said but I didn't. I got up and threw myself at him. I'm not brave. It wasn't that. It was the crack about looting and the way he stood posing.

He was ready for me. As I came at him he side-stepped and swung a terrific kick into my crotch. I collapsed half-conscious, gasping. He bent, grabbed my shirt and hauled me upright.

'There,' he hissed. 'Explained it more clearly have I, lad?' Gripping my arm, he half-ran me up the slope. We got to the top and he flung me from him. I tottered onto the downward slope, blind with tears. 'Go on,' he snarled. 'Piss off, and be thankful you weren't shot.'

A few yards down I stopped to get the water out of my eyes, and when I did I saw the hillside strewn with bodies and the town laid waste below.

SIX

They were everywhere. In the ditch, on the verge and on the road itself. Some didn't look bad; you could almost persuade yourself they were sleeping. Others were horrible, like the one by the pillbox.

At first, I peered at them as I passed; praying that none would turn out to be Mum or Dad or Ben. After a bit I couldn't stand it, so I didn't look any more, except to keep from falling over them. I walked like a blinkered horse, looking straight in front.

On the edge of town the houses were all burnt out, charred, glassless windows and caved-in roofs. Inside you could see wallpaper, fireplaces and bits of stairs going nowhere. Smoke rose thinly here and there through blackened timbers.

There was this old man, sitting in an armchair on the pavement. How it got there I don't know but there he was, staring at the wet flags. He was the first living person I'd seen all the way down and I crossed over and said, 'Are you all right?' It was a damn stupid thing to say but I wanted to hear his voice.

He didn't answer. He didn't even look up. He just went on staring at the pavement with his hands curled round the ends of the armrests. I repeated my question in a louder voice but there was no response; not even when I touched his shoulder. I guessed he must be in shock or something and I felt I ought to help – get him under cover perhaps. I looked about but all the houses were burnt and I couldn't see anybody else, so I left him.

As I moved further into town the damage got worse. Some of the buildings had collapsed; drifts of smashed brick lay spilled across the road and I had to pick my way round them. There were more bodies, and broken glass everywhere, some of it fused by heat into fantastic shapes. There were burnt out vehicles and the air smelled of charred wood.

Our shop was in the west part of town, the part farthest away from Branford. The worse devastation was to the east. As I made my way westward the damage grew lighter and I began to hope that I might find my family unscathed and my home intact.

I saw people. Some were walking about. Others sat on steps, gazing at the ground in front of them. Nobody looked at me, or tried to speak. I felt invisible, like a ghost.

Treading carefully between heaps of rubble and bits of glass I came to the top of my own street. Some of the houses still stood, others lay smashed. I could see from here that the shop was down.

I ran, in the middle of the road. My legs were weak with fear so that I almost fell.

The van lay on its side in the roadway, burnt out. The whole shop had collapsed though nearby houses still stood. I scrabbled among the rubble, calling brokenly to my parents. I imagined them lying crushed or burned beneath the bricks and plaster and I started to dig with my bare hands; pulling out bricks and throwing them aside. Then a voice said, 'Danny?' and I spun round, still bent over with a brick in either hand. My dad was standing by the cellar-steps, looking at me.

There was this angle of wall still standing: the kitchen corner where the cellar steps went down.

The bricks fell from my hands and I scrambled to him over the loose debris. He hugged me like he hadn't since I was a kid and I stood there sort of leaning on him, crying. My crotch hurt like hell.

I wiped my cheeks with the backs of my hands and said, 'Where's Mum and Ben?'

He looked down and shook his head. 'Your mother's gone, lad,' he said. 'She was up here, you see. Ben's in the cellar. He was down there with me when . . . he's asleep. We thought you were a goner, Danny. Where've you been?'

'The pillbox,' I told him. 'Up by Kershaw Farm. I went in out of the rain, and then I saw the flash. When I came out there were these men in rubber suits. One beat me up.'

'Beat you up?' he said. 'Why?'

'I don't know. They wouldn't tell me anything about what had happened and they made me leave the bike. I want to see Mum. Have you – ?'

'Aye,' he said quickly. 'I dug her out. Hoped she might be – you know, but it was no use. She's over there.' He nodded to where the counter sagged incongruously among bricks and twisted pipes. 'You don't want to see her, lad. Think of her as she was. She's wrapped up anyway.'

I gazed at him. Grey, stubbly face and pinkish eyes.

'Wrapped up?'

'Aye.' He wiped his palms on his coat and looked at the gutted houses across the road. 'It says in the booklet to wrap 'em up and tie a label on till they come to collect them. I had some polythene in the cellar but I can't find anything to write with so there's no label.'

I stared across at the counter. 'Who's coming?' I whispered. 'Them at Kershaw Farm?'

He shook his head. 'I don't know lad,' he said dully. 'It's been over a day already and I've not seen anyone. You can only do what it says and wait, can't you?'

I nodded, seeing the corpses on the hillside. Wondering who'd wrap them up and stick the labels on.

'Come on down.' He moved towards the steps. 'You must be starving. I'll get you some grub.'

The cellar was lit by two torches; one hanging from the light-flex and one clamped between two bags of sugar on a shelf. Dad had put down a strip of linoleum and Ben lay on it under a pile of blankets. He looked so peaceful, I wished I was seven.

SEVEN

Dad heated up a tin of sausage and beans for me. He'd made a cooker by cutting the top off an oil drum, filling it with sand and pouring paraffin into it. When he put a match to it, the surface of the sand burned with a blue flame. It stank, but it heated the food.

I ate ravenously, spoon in one hand and a hunk of stalish bread in the other. It didn't occur to me just then to wonder if the food was safe; I suppose I was too hungry.

It was no picnic though, all the same. The paraffin fumes stung my eyes and made me feel sick. I couldn't stop thinking about Mum. At the back of my mind lurked the question, 'How shall we live?' and, sub-consciously, I was saying, 'We won't. We'll die, every one of us, it's only a question of time.'

It was three nights since I'd slept properly and while I was eating a fantastic tiredness came over me. I said, 'I think I'd better turn in now if that's okay, Dad.' He was rummaging in a drawer and nodded without turning.

'All right, lad. I'll wake you about midnight so you can take your turn on guard.'

'What?' I thought I hadn't heard properly.

'Guard.' He pushed the drawer shut and straightened up with a stub of pencil in his hand. 'There's a lot of stock down here, Danny, and a lot of hungry people out there. We're lucky, but we've got to take care of our luck.'

There were two cellars; one for food and one for dry goods. Both were chock-full of stuff, enough to last three people years. I nodded. 'Oh, yes. Midnight then.'

I took my trainers off and got down beside Ben. It was hard, but there were plenty of blankets. Dad fetched a pick-handle from the other cellar and brandished it, grinning briefly. 'Had these in the army,' he growled. 'Guard duty. If it'll do for the army, it'll have to do for us. G'night, lad.'

He reached up and switched off the torch that dangled from the flex, then clumped away up the steps.

The beam of the remaining torch hit the white-washed ceiling and filled the cellar with a soft, reflected glow. Ben hadn't stirred: he lay with his mouth open, breathing gently. I envied him, but although I was utterly shattered I couldn't sleep. I lay gazing up at the flaky, cob-webbed ceiling while thoughts and speculations chased one another like the Keystone Cops across my mind.

How would we live? Who were those guys up at Kershaw Farm? Was that old fellow still sitting in his armchair under the stars?

It seemed like hours before I dropped off, and about five seconds later that Dad shook me. The torch still burned between the sugar bags. I found my shoes and tugged them on; the laces danced before my hot eyes as I fumbled with them. I stood up and Dad handed me the pick-handle.

'Been quiet,' he said. 'Too damn quiet. Keep your eyes skinned and give us a yell if you see owt.' He unbuttoned the shop-coat and hung it on a nail. I nodded and climbed out into the night.

EIGHT

He'd used rubble to make a sort of low wall across the corner. I moved to and fro behind it with the pick-handle in my hand or stood, straining my eyes into the dark. He was right: it was quiet. I don't think I'd ever known real quiet before. I mean, when you live in a town there's always noise, even in the middle of the night. You don't notice it but it's there. Real silence feels like something's pressing in on you, and so does darkness. It's never dark in town.

I was more tired than I'd ever been. My eyes ached and my body felt like it didn't belong to me. I kept taking these very deep breaths and hitting the side of my leg with the pick-handle to keep awake. I tried talking to myself but even a whisper sounded loud in the silence and I gave it up. I thought, maybe this is what it sounds like to be dead.

I thought about Mum, but it was unreal. Any other time I'd have wept for a week. I'd often imagined myself after her death, prostrate, clutching her picture, refusing food, wanting nothing of this world except to be shot of it and go to her. Maybe it was tiredness or shock or something, but it didn't feel like that at all. I was able to think about her in a detached way, as though she died a long time ago. I even thought, there she is, in a parcel under the counter like somebody's order, waiting to be collected.

It was a long night, but nothing happened. Eventually I

noticed that the sky to the east had paled and I could see the silhouettes of broken buildings against it. Imperceptibly, the paleness pearled and turned to faintest pink. It was cold, and all the smashed bricks had moisture on them. Soon, it was light enough for me to see that the street was empty. I laid my weapon on the wall and began breathing on my hands and rubbing them together. My feet were numb. I curled and flexed my toes over and over again till warmth came.

Presently I heard movements below and Dad came up, treading softly. There was a three-days growth of whiskers on his face. His chin was blue.

'All right?' His voice was low. I nodded.

'Quiet, like you said. Funny how shadows move when you're straining to see.' He laughed.

'You can say that again. Scare myself daft sometimes. By heck!' He rubbed his palms together. 'I'll be glad when that sun gets some heat in it. Somebody'll come today, I shouldn't wonder.'

'Aye.' My crotch was killing me and I thought about the man in the black outfit. 'I just hope they do summat for us when they do.'

Ben was still asleep. Dad went down again and came back with a big cardboard box. 'Here.' He set it down on the makeshift wall and handed me a tin-opener. 'Get cracking and open that lot while I find us something to drink.'

The box was full of tinned food, baked beans, spaghetti; stuff like that. There must have been twenty tins. I opened a couple, then waited till he came up again with some pop and sterilized milk. 'D'you want all these open?' I asked. He nodded and I said, 'Why? There's enough for about forty people here.' He nodded again. 'That's right. And it won't be long till there's forty waiting for it. We're not the only ones, y'know. Here.' He passed me a bottle of pop. Orangeade. I screwed the cap off, took a long swig and shivered. 'Ugh! Nice cup of coffee'd be more like it. Who're you feeding?'

He was quiet a minute, thinking. 'There's Mrs Troy and her lot, and that couple next to the filling-station, the Hansons. There's Les Holmes and his lad, his missus copped it like your mum. Then there's Mrs North from number sixty-three, the widow. And there's some others that I can't remember. A lot of folk still have stuff of their own, but they'll start running out in a day or two.'

I took another swig of the pop. 'Are we going to feed them all, everybody that comes?'

'Oh, no,' he said. 'Not everybody. Friends and neighbours, lad. Customers. It'll only be for a day or two, anyway.'

'We hope,' I said. 'But what if it isn't? What if nobody comes?'

He shrugged. 'They will, Danny. Bound to. But if they didn't, well, we'd just have to think again, wouldn't we?'

People started coming as soon as it was properly light. We gave them food and drink. Mrs Troy had four kids and no husband. One of the kids, Craig, was Ben's best friend. Ben was up when they arrived, and he wanted to go off with Craig but Dad said no. 'It's not safe,' he said. 'Buildings ready to fall down and funny people wandering about. You can play with Craig in a day or two, when the soldiers come.'

NINE

It sounds daft now, but we lived in hopes those first few days. We kept expecting somebody to come. Dad's booklet said the dead would be collected and feeding-centres set up. It said to listen to the radio; there'd be news, and instructions.

We knew there were people up at Kershaw Farm with fallout gear and weapons. People in authority. We assumed they were soldiers, and that they'd come down and start sorting things out like the soldiers in Turkey when there was that earthquake. In the meantime, we had to shift for ourselves.

A lot of people went mad. Not raving mad, but wandering aimlessly about in the ruins, muttering; or sitting absolutely still, staring at the ground.

You'd think people would've got together to organize tents and cooking and first-aid and that, but they didn't. They were stunned, I suppose. They'd be outside and it'd start to rain and they'd just stand or sit getting wet with places all round they could shelter in.

I think it was the ones who thought too much who went mad. I mean, if you went round thinking about how it was before and how you used to take it all for granted and that, I guess it could drive you daft. I think Dad realized that. He was always doing something, keeping himself busy so he hadn't time to brood about Mum and the shop and that.

What kept me going was Ben. You know how it is with little kids, some big change comes into their lives, a new school or moving house or something, and they're upset for maybe a couple of days. After that, they pick up their lives and carry on and it's like nothing's happened. They adjust to new situations with fantastic speed.

Ben was like that. I mean, one day he was this ordinary little lad, going off to school with his reading book and pencil case, coming home to watch telly and eat toffees and go to sleep in a warm bed; and the next he was a little survivor with no mum, living among ruins and sleeping on the floor. And he just did it. His mum wasn't buried three days before he was racing about in the rubble, playing soldiers. It was incredible. It kept me sane, watching him.

Nobody came, and there was only crackling on the radio, so Dad and me dug a hole in a garden opposite the shop and put Mum in it. It was raining. Dad said something he remembered from the Bible and rain ran down his face so you could only tell he was crying by his voice and you couldn't tell about me at all. It was evening, and Ben was asleep. We'd have shown him where she was later, only he never asked.

Water was a big problem. Tremors from Branford had fractured the mains and you saw bits of broken pipes sticking up out of the debris. A lot of people drank from puddles or collected rain in sheets of polythene, but we didn't. It was bound to be contaminated and, unlike other people, we had a choice. There was beer and pop in the cellar, and sterilized milk too. We drank that. Then somebody uncovered an old well in the yard of the Dog and Gun, and it became one of my jobs to fetch water twice a day in a tin bucket. It was while I was doing that one day that I first met Kim.

TEN

It was about three weeks after the bomb. A lot of the food and stuff which had been lying in houses had gone. Hunger-pains roused people from their stupor and they began asking when the help they'd been told to expect was going to materialize. Fights broke out, as those lucky enough to find food were set upon by their less fortunate fellows.

The situation was getting nastier every day. Ben was confined to the little triangle behind the wall, we'd used the counter and the wrecked van to strengthen it and make it higher. Ben, cooped up day and night, grizzled.

A group of people, a deputation they called themselves, set off up the road. They said they were off to Kershaw Farm to confront the soldiers and demand some relief for the town. They didn't return, and a rumour went round that shots had been heard.

Another bunch of survivors walked along the Branford road, intent on plundering a supermarket half a mile outside Skipley. They arrived at dusk to find the place under guard by armed men in fallout-suits. They watched from cover and saw a truck driven out, escorted by two men on motorbikes. The whole outfit headed for the moors.

That's how things were when I set off as usual with my bucket one evening in mid-September. What we'd do was, we'd get a bucketful in the morning to cook and brew tea, and another in the evening for washing. We even washed clothes for a time.

Anyway, I was heading for the Dog and Gun. You had to go up our street, turn left at the top and it was about a quarter of a mile.

Suddenly, someone cried out nearby. The sound seemed to come from a narrow street leading off, and I ran to the end to look.

Coming towards me was a girl. She was running clutching the strap of a plastic sports-bag which swung and bounced against her leg as she ran. Two lads were chasing her, one had a length of heavy chain and the other a whip-aerial off a car.

I'm no hero, and the last thing I wanted right then was a fight. My crotch was still pretty sore, but the lass was only about five yards from me with the two lads close behind. I was dangling the bucket, and as the girl ran past I swung it at the nearest lad. It caught him on the side of the head and he fell. The other one swerved round me and went after the girl. I flung the bucket at his back and set off after him.

The girl was halfway down the street. Her green skirt flew as she ran and the bag bounced against her leg. The lad was gaining on her. As I pelted after them he raised the aerial and swiped her across the shoulder with it. She cried out, swerved and tried to scramble up a mound of smashed bricks. The rubble shifted and she slipped. The lad darted in and seized the bag but the girl held on to the strap. He tugged on the bag and slashed at her repeatedly but she hung on, shielding her head with her free arm.

He was so intent on getting the bag that he didn't look to see where I was till I was nearly on top of him. I snatched up a half-brick and, as he turned, flung it. He clapped both hands to his face. Blood spurted from between his fingers and ran over his hands.

I grabbed the girl by an arm and tried to drag her away.

'No, wait!'

She pulled herself free, bent down and pulled something out of the rubble. It was a bit of iron railing; one of those old ones with a spear tip. The lad I'd clobbered sat curled up, holding his face.

I didn't know what she intended to do until she dropped her bag and lifted the spike above her head with both hands. I stood gaping till it was almost too late then flung myself at her, knocking her sideways and falling on top of her. The rail flew out of her hand and slithered away down the mound. The lad scrambled to his feet and tottered off, holding his face.

I glanced at the long spike, then at the girl. She'd wriggled herself out from underneath me and was knocking dirt off her sleeve. She looked angry. I said, 'You wouldn't have done it, would you, killed him, just like that?'

She glared at me, tight-lipped; straightening her dress. Then her features softened and she said, 'It's going to be us or them, you know.' She picked up the bag and stood dangling it, looking down at me. 'Come on.'

I picked myself up and looked around. Both lads had gone and I said, 'See. You didn't have to be *that* drastic.'

She smiled and I looked at her. She was thin with long, pale hair. Fourteen or so. She had this green dress; thin stripes of white and green really – a school dress, and sandals. Her toes and the tops of her feet were dirty. She seemed nice, which is a crazy thing to say after what she'd meant to do.

Anyway, she said, 'Had a good look, have you?'

I felt my face going red and I said, 'What were they after you for?'

She held up the bag. 'This.'

'What's in it?' I asked. She gave me this incredulous look.

'Food of course. What else?'

Instead of answering I said, 'My name's Danny: what's yours?'

'Kim.'

'Where d'you live?'

She gave a vague wave. 'Over there.'

'Which street?' I persisted.

'Victoria Place,' she said. 'Why?'

I shrugged. 'Just wondered. Will you be all right now?'

She gave a short laugh. 'Sure. Will you?'

'I mean, d'you want me to walk along with you?'

She looked at me coolly. 'Haven't you got your own problems?'

I shrugged again. 'I guess so. But I could see you home if you like.'

'How come you're not after my grub. Or maybe you are?'

'No!' I blurted, angrily. 'I don't need it, we've got a shop.'

As soon as I'd said it I knew I shouldn't have. Dad would have called it drawing attention to our luck. Be thankful for it, he kept saying, but don't draw attention to it.

She must have read the look on my face because she said, 'It's okay. I don't need your stuff either, there's a place I know near Branford.'

'What's it like?' I asked.

'What?'

'Branford.' Talking to her was making me feel real for the first time in days and I didn't want her to go. I said, 'Let's walk towards your place, we can talk as we go.'

She looked at me for a moment without speaking. Then she shrugged and said, 'Okay. But one wrong move and I split, right?'

I nodded. 'Okay.'

We started walking. The sun had dipped below the broken roofs and dusk was seeping through the little streets. 'You want to know what Branford's like?' she said. 'Gone, that's what it's like. One big bomb, one big hole, no Branford.'

'No survivors?'

She shook her head. 'Shouldn't think so. Hole must be fifty feet deep. I've been close four times and I've never seen anybody alive.'

I kicked a lump of brick. 'Two-hundred-thousand people. I wonder who'll tie all the labels on?'

She glanced at me sidelong. 'You don't believe all that stuff, do you?'

'What stuff?'

'What it says in the book.'

I shrugged. 'I was joking about the labels, but somebody'll come eventually.'

She grinned briefly, swinging her bag. 'Who? The enemy? The guys who did this?' They're in the same boat we're in, Danny-boy.'

'No.' I jerked my head towards the moor. 'Them. The soldiers, or whatever they are. They'll come and sort things out.'

'Why?' There was a mocking light in her eyes.

'Because it's their job,' I snapped. 'That's why. Soldiers always step in where there's a disaster.'

'You're joking!' She swung the bag in a full circle. 'Would *you* come down into this lot if you were sitting up there on the moor in your protective gear on top of a bunkerful of clean grub?' She laughed. 'They're only people you know, like you and me. They want to survive, just like us. You don't think they're about to get all that uncontaminated grub out and start dishing it up to us, do you?'

I shrugged again to hide my unease. The vanished deputation. The shots. What she was saying seemed to be borne out by what had happened up to now.

'I don't know, Kim,' I said. 'It's taking them a long time, but I can't believe they'd just leave us to die.'

'Can't you?' She looked at me sideways. 'I'll tell you something, Mister. If they were down here and I was up there, I'd leave *them* to die, no danger.' She stopped. 'Anyway, this is where I live.'

It was a burnt-out house in a terrace of burnt-out houses. I grinned. 'Better than us,' I said. 'We've only got a cellar.'

'Oh, aye,' she rejoined. 'But it's full of grub though, isn't it?' Her eyes still mocked.

'Look.' I gazed at the cobbles, shuffling my feet. 'I – can we see each other again? Where d'you get your water?'

She grinned. 'Dog and Gun, same as you. Only my sister goes for it.'

'Can you come instead? Tomorrow night?'

She shrugged. 'Dunno. Have to see, won't we? I've got to go in now.'

She turned and walked up the path. There was a charred door. She slapped it with her open hand, twice. It opened. I peered through the gathering twilight, trying to see the sister. There was only a pale blob against the darkness inside. On the step, Kim turned and called softly, 'G'night. Thanks for the rescue act.' Then she was gone, and I said my goodnight to the blackened door.

ELEVEN

That night, lying with Ben in the cellar, I couldn't stop thinking about Kim. It was crazy. I mean, I'd known girls I'd liked before, but not so they kept me awake. I lay thinking of things I should have said. I wished I'd been cool or witty or something, instead of stammering. I hadn't even managed to say good-night before she shut the door for God's sake. The more I went over it in my head, the dafter my performance appeared and the more convinced I became that I'd never see her again. What a twit I'd been, what a pillock.

The fact that she'd been about to kill a bloke was sort of swamped by all these other feelings, and it wasn't hard to find excuses. We were in a new game. The old rules no longer applied. There were no rules in this game; only the ones we made up as we went along. Maybe Kim was better suited to the new game than I was. Maybe I'd had no right to stop her.

I was on guard the last half of the night and I was shattered. I'd hardly slept thinking of Kim and I went on thinking about her as I stood half-frozen, peering into the dark, holding the shotgun Dad had got from somewhere. I kept looking towards Victoria Place, and every time I did I got this ache in my chest. I was like one of those love-lorn prannocks in an old movie.

Anyway, next morning began as usual. Dad came up with the cooker and his shaving-tackle. He was the last clean-shaven guy in Skipley. I went for water. I knew Kim wouldn't be there. I kept a lookout for anybody who might be her sister, but the only woman I saw was more like someone's granny. We heated the water and I took Ben's breakfast down to him. He always had this cereal with hot powdered milk. Dad and I ate ours outside and then he shaved sitting hunched forward on his chair, looking into a bit of broken mirror propped up on mine.

Looking back it was a weird time, that first three weeks after the bomb. It was unreal. At least, it felt unreal to me and I suppose it was the same for everybody. One life had ended and the next hadn't begun. We tried to cling to the old life but it slipped away and we drifted in limbo, waiting. That day, the day after I met Kim, was the end of waiting and first day of the new life.

It started after breakfast. We'd washed the bowls and spoons and Ben had stowed them in the cellar. Dad lugged out a big square of canvas and we stood on chairs and draped it over the brickwork so that it made an awning across our little triangle. It sagged in the middle. Dad thought rain might gather there and drag the whole thing down so he pulled some lengths of timber out of the rubble to use like tent-poles. I'd just started digging holes for them when we heard the loud-speaker.

At first it was so far off you couldn't tell which direction it was coming from. I was hitting the ground with the spade when Dad flapped a hand at me. 'Sssh!'

We listened, straining our ears. There was a quacking in the distance like a tin duck and Ben laughed out loud. Dad pressed a finger to his lips and Ben stifled his giggles. The sound came nearer, separating out into warped, unintelligible words.

Somewhere, people started to shout. Dad turned, his eyes shining. 'It's them!' he breathed. 'The soldiers. It must be!' He scooped Ben up in his arms and vaulted with him over the counter. I flung the spade aside and followed. We stood at the roadside, gazing up the street.

Round the corner came a blue car with a loudspeaker on its roof. And after it, whooping and capering in their rags, came a throng of people.

As the procession approached I felt a lump in my throat and my eyes filled with tears. They ran down my cheeks and I didn't care. I remembered a bit of newsreel I saw once; the Allies entering Paris in 1944. People threw flowers. I knew now how they must have felt and I wished I had flowers to throw.

The vehicle was moving at walking speed and as it drew level, it stopped. Its windows were of darkened glass; its occupants dim shapes within. There was a click and the loudspeaker crackled.

'We represent your Local Commissioner,' it said. 'Stand by for a Special Instruction.' There was a brief interval, during which the vehicle's motley escort clapped and cheered. The broadcast continued.

'An emergency hospital has been set up, adjacent to Local Commission Headquarters at Kershaw Farm, and a fleet of ambulances is following this vehicle. Will those of you who are able-bodied please see to it that all burned, sick and badly injured persons are brought out of buildings and placed at the roadside. Please note that only serious cases will be dealt with. Persons suffering from minor injuries will be treated in due course. That is all.'

The car moved on, amid a fresh burst of cheering. I followed it to the bottom of the street then walked back, buoyant with relief. Knots of people were emerging from the ruins, carrying their sick and wounded. Soon the street was lined with them, slumped in arm-chairs or lying on doors and mattresses while relatives hovered near, waiting for the ambulances.

I was amazed how many people there were. Most of them must have remained hidden for the past three weeks in the shells of their houses, because I'd seen very few on the streets or round the well, and the number coming to us for food had hardly altered.

Dad had returned to the job of erecting the poles. I joined him, working happily now that the worst was over. Little Craig Troy appeared and he and Ben played together in the rubble, their shrill voices in our ears as we worked.

It was over an hour before the first ambulance appeared. It wasn't an ambulance, but a canvas-covered military truck with red crosses painted crudely on its sides. It worked its way slowly down the street, stopping every few yards to pick up casualties. As the injured were lifted aboard, relatives clamoured round the tailboard, asking questions in loud, excited voices. When might they visit? How long would this or that patient be gone? What about the dead? All questions were met with shrugs, shaken heads or tinny don't knows.

When the truck was full, the tailboard was slammed shut and the vehicle sped away, scattering spectators. Groans and exclamations followed it from the relatives of those left behind, but shortly afterwards a second truck appeared, and when it eventually rumbled away round the corner, no casualties remained in our street.

People hung about for a while, talking. Dad and I put the finishing touches to our awning, while Ben and his playmate played at soldiers and casualties with a cardboard box for a truck. If they'd known what was happening up at Kershaw Farm, they'd have played at something else.

TWELVE

If the soldiers hadn't come it would have been a long day. I'd have hung around thinking of Kim, worrying myself daft over whether she'd turn up at the well or not. As it was, it was evening before I knew it.

I got the bucket and walked up the street, happier than I'd been since the bomb. Happier than I was before it in a way, because before the bomb I didn't know I was happy.

As I walked, I thought about the people up at the hospital. For three weeks they'd waited in the ruins famished, cold, in pain. We'd heard their cries in the night, but there'd been nothing we could do. Now I pictured them in rows of warm, clean beds; their wounds dressed and their hunger satisfied; drifting to sleep under nurses' watchful eyes. Even those with radiation sickness, who were sure to die, would slip away easily, their minds numbed with sedatives.

And that wasn't all, I told myself. Soon, the less grievously injured would be taken care of; perhaps they'd set up clinics where you'd be able to go, even if you only had toothache or something. And after that there'd be feeding-centres, like it said in the book, with hot meals for all. No need to sit up half the night, guarding the stock.

It made a comfortable picture. I remember I sighed as I imagined it. And the fact that I was on my way to see Kim was the icing on my cake.

She hadn't arrived when I got there. There were two guys in the cobbled yard. I loitered by the archway that led into the yard.

I was just beginning to worry when I turned, and she was there. Same dress, dangling a bucket. Something turned over in my chest and my face burned.

'Oh, hi Kim,' I said lightly. This time I'd be cool.

'Hello,' she said. 'Been waiting long?'

'Just got here. Thought you'd been and gone.' Cool.

She shrugged. 'What were you hanging about for, then?'

'Waiting for them.' I nodded towards the two men. They were coming through the arch with their water.

We went through into the yard. I stood watching as she lowered the bucket. There was this bucket that was there all the time. It was on a rope. You hauled the water up in that and tipped it into your own. When she had the bucket full I took hold of the rope. She didn't let go and we pulled together, our hands and hips touching. The rope could have been two miles long and the bucket would still have come up too soon for me.

My run of luck wasn't over, either, because when I started to haul my own water up she took hold and pulled with me. Hand and hip. Cool on the surface, hot inside.

'Think I'll walk back your way,' I said, casually.

She smiled. 'Miles out of your way,' she mocked. 'Nobody waiting for the water?'

'Dad,' I said. 'He can wait.' I went to pick up both buckets. She grabbed hers and pulled it away, slopping a little.

'I can manage,' she said. 'I'm not paralysed, you know.'

I shrugged. 'Being a gentleman, that's all.'

'Haven't you heard,' she said. 'Gentlemen are out. Cavemen rule, okay?'

We left the yard.

Her crack about cavemen had reminded me of the soldiers. I said, 'You were wrong about the soldiers: they did come.' I looked sideways at her. The water was heavy and she walked tilted over to the right. She frowned.

'They came,' she said. 'But don't you think it was a bit funny?'

'What, taking the casualties away? What's funny about it?'

'There's this old couple,' she said. 'Next door but one. The old woman's burned all down one side. We took her out this morning, and they loaded her in with a lot of others. The old guy was upset. Maureen, that's my sister, asked when he could go up and visit his wife. The soldiers just shook their heads. Didn't say any time, or that visiting isn't allowed or anything. And when she asked again they sort of pushed her aside and moved off. It didn't seem right to me.'

'They'll be fantastically busy,' I said. 'There must be thousands of casualties. There'll be no time for frills like visiting.'

'That's another thing.' She kicked a stone and watched it skip along the flags. 'How the heck do they intend to look after thousands of people? What sort of hospital can you build in three weeks? I think they had something to hide, and that's why they wouldn't answer Maureen.'

'Rubbish!' I hadn't meant to talk to her like that, but she seemed intent on messing up what till now had been a perfect day. I was about to tell her so when a commotion broke out behind us. We turned.

A man was coming along the street. A cripple. He dragged one leg and hung onto things, moving in a series of jerky swoops from one support to the next; shouting in this high, cracked voice. He was too far off for us to make out what he was saying.

As we watched, a couple of men came out and grabbed him and sat him down on the bonnet of a burnt-out car. He went on shouting, waving his arms about and trying to get up. One of the men called out and a woman came running. The man said something to her and she sank down on the pavement with her hands over her ears, shaking her head.

'Something's happened!' cried Kim. 'Come on.' She put down the bucket and began running back towards the group round the car.

I stood gazing after her while dread spread like cold water across my guts. I couldn't move. I remember thinking: Perhaps if I stand very still it'll be all right. It'll be all right.

I didn't even put the bucket down. She looked back when she reached the car but she was too far away for me to see the expression on her face.

She was talking to them. The men on the bonnet had quietened down but the woman still sat doubled up on the ground. Kim bent and touched her hands but she didn't respond. Kim started walking towards me, slowly, till I could see her eyes. They weren't looking at me. They weren't looking at anything. When she came up to me she didn't speak, but lifted the bucket and walked on. I transferred mine to the other hand and hurried after her.

When we came to her gateway, she turned in without speaking and I called after her, 'Kim?' The cake had crumbled into dust and the icing was melting.

She stopped and turned. When she spoke her voice was dead, like her eyes.

'They shot them, Danny,' she said. 'Every one of them. People heard shots and ran up the road. They saw an earth-mover and some pits. Guys in fallout-suits opened fire on them. That man back there got clear.' She paused, biting her lip and gazing at the ground. 'That won't be the end of it,' she continued in the same, flat voice. 'Now that they've killed off the sick, they'll be after somebody else – old people maybe, or kids. And after that, somebody else and somebody else, till it comes down to us. Us or them.' She looked me up and down, assessing my chances. 'Cavemen versus gentlemen is no contest,' she said. 'We've got to be as hard as they are, Danny boy – or harder. See you.'

I stood watching till the door closed, then made my way homeward in the dusk. Fires flickered in some of the houses. Cooking smells hung on the air and I caught fragments of conversation. Somebody played a mouth-organ, and a loud guffaw burst out from the darkness beyond a frameless window.

I pictured them, these invisible people, happy as I had been, imagining their loved ones safe and warm. Knowing the reality, the sick, going to their deaths with our cheering in their ears, I attempted indifference. Compassion belonged to the old life. Hardness was the thing.

So they're dead, I hissed. So what?

Then I thought about this old man, waiting for his wife to come home, and how she was beautiful to him, even though she was just an ugly old woman. He'd wait and wait and never see her again, even though he'd wait forever if he could. And I started to cry, and trailed along humping the bucket while tears ran down my face. Cavemen versus gentlemen. Hardness versus compassion. No contest.

THIRTEEN

You'd expect that when the news got round the scene would turn ugly. You might even expect some sort of revolt, a mass-attack on Kershaw Farm or something of that sort.

I expected it. I lay in bed that night and wondered what would happen when all the people in Skipley stormed the hill. Not if – when!

It never happened. All that happened was a lot of shouting and crying, and a few people set off up the hill with sticks and stuff. The soldiers had anticipated it and the marchers found themselves facing an APC. That's an armoured personnel carrier, like a little tank with machine-guns. They had no leader and no plan, so they chucked their sticks away and ran.

I was fantastically depressed. Everybody was. We'd waited and waited for someone to come and help us. We'd had our hopes raised, and now it was back to square one. It was worse than if it had never happened!

Even Ben was affected. He didn't know what was going on, but he found himself confined once more behind the wall. Dad said people would get desperate and he didn't want the kid running about.

He was right, too. There was a new feeling in the air – a tension, as though something awful was building up and might explode at any moment. When I went to the well, I carried a club and when I got there somebody had taken the bucket. I had to scrat about in the rubble for something to tie to my own, and all the time I felt as though I was being watched, as though I was stealing somebody else's water. I found something in the end, a length of TV cable, and I got some water. I coiled the cable round my waist before I left the yard. Before, I'd have left it for the next guy, but if somebody had pinched the bucket they'd probably take that, too.

That wasn't the worst thing, though. The worst thing was when I found out that some people had known there was no hospital. It was a few days later, I was under the arch and I heard two blokes and a woman talking.

'Well; it was pretty obvious, wasn't it,' one of them said. 'I mean, it's like the Nazis. As soon as I heard it over the loud-speaker I said to myself, "Aye – it's like the Nazis with their gas vans." ' The others nodded.

'Yes,' said the woman, 'We'd a fair idea ourselves but what could we do? She was covered in burns, and it's bad enough finding grub for two . . .'

That's the worst thing – you get so that you'll send your own folk off to die, thinking, sooner them than us.

FOURTEEN

Things were getting harder. For one thing it was October, and we'd had the first touch of frost. Tents and makeshift shelters had sprung up among the ruins. The last scraps of food had disappeared from the empty houses and now they were being stripped of bedding, carpets and bits of linoleum. Clothes were taken from the ruins and from the dead, and we presented a bulky appearance because of the many layers we wore.

The air of tension had intensified, and was made worse by the long silence from Kershaw Farm. We'd expected another visit from the loudspeaker and listened for it, subconsciously, as we went about our work. Nothing happened.

I hadn't seen Kim again. Fetching water had become a perilous chore and I didn't hang about. I kept to the middle of the road and moved quickly, with the bucket in one hand and a club in the other; watching the ruins on either side as I went. The length of cable was coiled about my waist, hidden under my clothes.

If there were people at the well I waited under the arch with my back against the wall. My evening trips got earlier and earlier as the nights drew in – I had to be home before dusk. Some people only made one trip now, in the mornings, and I'd have done the same if I hadn't always kept hoping I'd see Kim. There seemed more chance, going twice a day, but we were never there at the same time. I began to think something had happened to her.

It wouldn't have been surprising if something had. More and more people were dying of the sickness, and every night some poor devil was done in for his clothes or any grub he might have about him.

The first new words emerged. One morning at the well I heard some man refer to the mad men and women who wandered through the ruins, talking to themselves or calling to lost relatives. Spacers, he called them. And I'd heard a few people call those dying of the sickness, terminals. They were only words, but they made me uneasy. If you call people things like that, it makes them seem less than human somehow.

A few mornings later I heard another, though I didn't recognise it for what it was. Badgers. This man said he knew where there were some badgers, and did the other bloke fancy helping dig them out?

The other guy said no, and they started arguing. Then they noticed me and one of them, the one who knew where the badgers were, came over. I gripped my club and eyed him warily.

'How about you?' He growled. 'D'you fancy giving me a hand?'

I shrugged. 'I don't know,' I said. 'Are badgers okay to eat?' He laughed. 'We don't eat the badgers,' he said. 'Not the badgers: we're not down to that yet. But we eat what they've got in their holes, don't we Ken?'

He glanced over his shoulder at the man by the well, who shook his head and murmured, 'You do, Charlie, not me.'

'Aye,' agreed Charlie. 'I do. How about it, kiddo?'

I didn't know what to say. The man seemed to be offering me a chance to get food. I didn't need it, but I didn't want him to know that. On the other hand, I was pretty sure badgers didn't store food. 'I don't know,' I said again.

He made an exasperated noise and spread his hands. 'Look kid,' he said, 'I'm making you an offer. Give us a hand you'll get your share of the stuff. It'll take us maybe an hour, and it'll be the easiest grub you ever won, okay?'

I held up my bucket. 'I've got to take water home, my dad's waiting.'

'Be my guest.' He stepped aside and indicated the well with a sweep of his hand. 'Take the water home, and come back here. You'll be glad you did.'

The second chap had filled his bucket. He came out through the arch and as he passed us, his eyes found mine and he shook his head, ever so slightly. Charlie saw the gesture and laughed again. 'Get on with you, Ken!' he bellowed. 'You're soft, that's your trouble. You'll end up with your skull bashed in, or else you'll starve!'

Soft. Kim's words echoed in my head. *We've got to be as hard as they are, Danny boy.* I looked at Charlie.

'Okay,' I said. 'I'll see you back here as soon as I can.' He grinned. 'Right you are, kiddo,' he said. 'Only don't take too long, or somebody else'll find my ruddy badgers!'

FIFTEEN

I didn't say anything to Dad about Charlie. I told him I had to see somebody. He told me to be careful.

Charlie was waiting under the arch. He'd been off somewhere in the meantime, because he had some stuff with him; a bulging carrier-bag and a sort of canister with a nozzle.

'What's that?' I asked.

'For making smoke. Come on.' He set off at a brisk pace up the road. I followed with my club.

We made for the west end of town – a place of large, expensive houses and tree-lined avenues. Damage was light here, but there was nobody about. I thought we were going to Calverley Wood, where badgers were sometimes seen, but we weren't. Charlie led me into a road over-arched with scorched horse-chestnut trees and there, by the gateway to a house, we stopped.

'This is it,' he growled. A concrete driveway led up to some garage doors. Charlie walked up it and I followed, feeling uneasy. It didn't seem likely to me that badgers would make their home in somebody's garden. I was beginning to wish I hadn't come. The other guy had refused, and he'd tried to warn me. Why?

I suppose I could have run off, but I didn't. I followed Charlie along a pathway between the garage and the side of the house.

There was a large garden at the back: lawns mostly, with a high wall and old trees round. It must have been nice before, but the grass was yellow now and the trees had a shrivelled look.

'Where're the badgers?' I whispered.

Charlie had dropped the bag on the path and was doing something to the canister. He pressed a warning finger to his lips, then pointed across the garden. There was a lawn, then a sort of bank about three feet high and another lawn beyond that. Stone steps led from one to the other. In the middle of the far lawn was a slab of concrete about the size of a snooker table. Charlie had pointed to that. I looked at it, then down at him.

'What is it?' I whispered. A dark suspicion was forming in my mind. He glanced up, fiddling with matches.

'Shelter.'

I went cold. 'You mean – ?'

'Aye.' Smoke rose from the nozzle. He straightened. I backed off, gripping the club. He stuffed the matches in a jacket pocket and left his hand there. I shook my head.

'No,' I whispered. 'I can't. Badgers, you said. I'm going.'

'Like fun you are!' His hand, wrapped round a small pistol, rose from his pocket. 'It's a two-man job, kiddo. You do your bit, or die: it's as simple as that.' His voice hadn't risen above a low growl, but there was no doubting his earnestness. He nodded towards my club. 'Drop that.'

I dropped it, and he said, 'Get the smoker.' He backed away and I bent, lifting it by its handle.

'Right.' He pointed to the thing with his free hand. 'All you do is, you squeeze there when you want smoke to come out. You do it when I say, and you keep on till I say stop. And remember.' He held the gun under my nose. 'I'll be watching you.'

He picked up the bag and we crossed the lawn to the steps. He made me go up first. Two short pipes protruded from the concrete; one at either end. Charlie thrust his mouth close to my ear.

'You stand by that one. When I nod my head, you shove the

nozzle in and start squeezing. And whatever happens, keep on going; if you stop before I tell you, you're dead, right?' I nodded.

He moved to the far end and began pulling rags from the carrier. The pistol lay beside him in the grass. When he had a pile, he squatted and started stuffing them into the pipe. I stood, wishing I'd heeded the man called Ken.

He rammed in the last of the rags, dropped the bag over the pipe and picked up the gun. He held it up in front of him and closed one eye, peering along the snub barrel with the other. Then he lowered it, grinned across at me, and nodded.

I pushed the nozzle into the pipe and started to pump. Charlie came over and squatted on his heels, smiling to himself and toying with the gun.

For a while nothing happened and I began to think, maybe there's nobody down there. Maybe the owners were away when the bomb fell.

Then I heard a noise: a muffled exclamation, followed by coughing.

I looked across at Charlie and shook my head; a sort of mute appeal. He raised the pistol, gazed balefully at me along its barrel, and nodded.

Choking sounds came from below, like voices from the grave. My limbs trembled and I felt sick. Charlie was still pointing the gun at me and I went on squeezing, while cold sweat trickled down my back.

There was a new sound; a grinding, mechanical noise, and a square trap in the centre of the concrete lifted slightly. The choking sounds grew clearer and smoke poured out. Charlie crept forward till he was directly behind the trap.

It swung back, and through the smoke the head and shoulders of a man appeared. Choking, the man staggered out onto the concrete with his hands over his eyes. Charlie raised the pistol.

I didn't stop to think. If I had, I wouldn't have done it. I pulled the nozzle out of the pipe, ran across the pad and hit Charlie as hard as I could with the canister.

He toppled sideways and, flinging the smoker from me, I

grabbed his wrist and wrenched the gun from his grasp. I'd hoped he'd be knocked out but he wasn't. He rolled, making a grab for my ankle as I leapt clear.

'Hold it!' The man spun round, his eyes streaming. His jaw dropped. 'Stand still!' I cried, and glanced at Charlie. He was kneeling on the concrete with his hand pressed to his ear. 'You!' I jabbed the gun at him. 'Get up and stand with him. Move away from the hatch.'

Sounds of distress issued from the shelter. I looked at the man. 'Tell 'em to come out.'

He was looking at Charlie and me as though we were ghosts. Maybe he'd expected no survivors on the surface. Without taking his eyes off me he called hoarsely, 'Lynne. Come up here. Bring Rebecca.'

Smoke was still rising from the hatch. A woman's head appeared. She staggered up the steps, blind with tears, carrying a kid of three or so. The kid had puked down her jumper. When she saw me, the woman screamed and sort of turned, shielding the kid.

'Okay,' I rapped. 'Nobody'll hurt you. Charlie?'

He glared at me, nursing his ear.

'Go on down and get what we came for. I'll watch these.'

'Get 'em shot!' he growled. 'Never mind watching 'em.'

'No,' I said. 'There's no need. Get the stuff and let's go.'

He shook his head. 'I'm not off down there,' he said. 'He can go.' He nodded towards the man.

'All right.' I turned to him. 'Go down,' I said. 'Fetch up any food you've got down there – also blankets, clothes and anything else you can carry. Make it quick.'

The man moved towards the hatch. 'Oh, and think on,' I said. 'Any funny business and the woman gets it.' He nodded and went down.

Charlie's lip curled. 'The woman gets it,' he sneered. 'You're flamin' soft, kiddo; you couldn't do it!'

'Maybe not,' I snapped. 'To her. But I'll do it to you if you give me half an excuse.'

The child had been sick again and was crying. The woman set it down on the grass and worked on it with a tissue. The man dumped a cardboard box on the pad, glanced towards his family and ducked down again. The last of the smoke had dispersed.

He made four trips. The fourth time he lugged an armful of bedding up. 'That's all,' he said. I nodded and he climbed out.

I looked at the stuff. A few tins of grub, a radio and a torch. Blankets, clothes and batteries. Charlie had been prepared to kill three people for this stuff, and there must be a hundred times as much in our cellar. I shivered, then got a hold of myself.

'Okay, Charlie,' I said. 'Pick it up.' I covered the family while he sorted the stuff out. I'd no idea how the gun worked, I probably couldn't have fired it if I'd wanted to. They stood in a huddle on the lawn, watching me.

Charlie said, 'Right, kiddo: now what?' He was half-hidden behind a pile of blankets. I jerked my head towards the pathway. 'You set off. I'll cover you.' I turned from him and gazed levelly into the man's eyes. 'If you try to come after us, I'll kill you.'

'Kill 'em anyway!' called Charlie, halfway across the lawn. I started to follow him, walking backwards and watching the family. They gazed back impassively, not stirring. I turned away.

There was a loud bang. Charlie, on the top step, shot forward, arms outflung. I whirled. The family hadn't moved, but another man stood on the shelter-steps, a shotgun smoking in his hands. I dropped, and the second shot passed over me, knocking pebble-dash from the house-wall. Two barrels, two shots. I sprang up and leapt for the steps.

Charlie at the bottom sprawled among blankets, wetly red. Tins of beans on the grass. I ran.

That night, back on guard again, I couldn't get it out of my head. Standing there with Dad's gun, waiting to make a Charlie out of somebody. Would I, I wondered, if it came to it? Shoot 'em anyway, says Charlie in my skull. We've got to be as hard as they are, says Kim.

Anyway, that's what badgers were: people in shelters. Charlie wasn't the only one hunting them. One by one, they were found, smoked out and shot for their stuff – for their selfishness too, perhaps, ('You can lob 'em over now, Ivan, I've got a shelter.'), until there were none left.

Spacers, badgers, terminals. Three new species. Better than shooting people.

SIXTEEN

We lost count of time after a while. There was no radio or TV, and all the public clocks had either fallen or stopped. There were watches and house-clocks but nothing to check them against. We still looked at our watches and said, 'It's ten o'clock' or 'It's dinner-time,' but it wasn't really, everybody's time was different.

It was the same with days and dates. You might think it's impossible for everybody to forget what day it is, but it's easy once there's no work to go to or appointments to keep. I fancied they'd be keeping accurate time up at Kershaw Farm, and maybe there was somebody somewhere cutting notches in a pole like Robinson Crusoe, but the rest of us lost track within a few weeks and the whole system disintegrated.

We took to estimating time by the sun's position, the pains in our bellies, and the quality of the light.

I don't know when it was, therefore, that the blue car appeared again. I know it was morning, and stunningly cold, and that the tinny quack of the loudspeaker carried a long way on the frigid air.

A combination of factors had weakened us: the onset of winter, the death of optimism, the growth of fear. Nobody hurried towards the long-anticipated sound. There was no capering throng, and no cheering. We paused in our tasks, glanced into one-another's eyes and moved without unnecessary speed to the roadside where we stood, looking deceptively fat in our layers of shabby clothes.

The car crunched down the trash-strewn, hoary street, followed by a drab-green APC. Both vehicles stopped and the loudspeaker clicked.

'We represent your Local Commissioner,' said the voice.

'Aye,' muttered a woman close to me. 'We know.'

'Stand by for a Special Instruction.' We stood by.

'In response to the acute shortages of food and fuel within his area, the Commissioner has drawn up a system of rationing which he proposes to put into immediate effect.' The speaker paused. There was a shuffling of cold feet and somebody coughed.

'A registration-point has been set up at the council offices in Market Square. It will be manned for the next three days, and a ration-card will be issued to each person who presents himself for registration. Parents or guardians of children must take their children with them in order to obtain child ration cards. No card will be issued to one person for use by another. Issue of food rations will commence on the morning following the final registration day, a field-kitchen having been set up for this purpose in Ramsden Park. Vehicles will tour the town over the next few days, collecting food and fuel for fair distribution, and you are advised that as of now, the hoarding or concealment of food and fuel is an offence carrying severe penalties. You are urged to co-operate with the Authority in the interest of national recovery. That is all.'

The vehicles moved on. The woman who had spoken before said, 'What the heck do they think we've got here; coal-dumps and supermarkets or what?'

'I don't trust 'em,' a man replied. 'Not after that hospital gag. They're getting nowt out of me.'

'Aye,' said another. 'We co-operated with authority all our lives and look where it got us.' He indicated the broken town with a sweep of his arm and sounds of agreement greeted the gesture.

The gathering began to break up. Dad and Ben had gone already, and I was about to follow them when I heard somebody say, 'I hope those Lodges'll turn their stock over all the same: they've enough stuff down there to feed an army.'

I glanced round. A knot of people lingered nearby, looking in my direction. I looked away quickly and went towards the shop. I didn't like what I'd heard, but I couldn't really blame them. Dad had doled out his stuff to a chosen few while the majority went hungry, and he couldn't expect to be the most popular man in town. Still, there was a new situation now. People were going to be fed regularly, including us. There was no need to hoard the stuff any longer, and I took it for granted he'd turn it over to the Authority.

I was wrong, though. As soon as I was back under the awning he said, 'Those people out there were right – a man'd be a fool to trust 'em with his stuff.'

I looked at him. 'Some of them were talking about us just now,' I said. 'And there's no way they're going to let us get away with it, Dad. If we don't turn it in they'll shop us.'

'Who?' he demanded. 'Who's going to shop us? What good would that do 'em?'

I shrugged. 'It won't do them any good, Dad – they'll do it out of envy. And even if they don't, those people aren't daft. This was a shop – they'll know we've got stuff stashed away.'

'Well –' He jerked his head towards the cellar. 'There's a perfectly good double-barrelled shotgun down there, and you've got that pistol. We've held our patch up to now and we'll go on holding it.'

'But Dad!' I cried. 'We've held it against unarmed people who're sick and weak. We're talking about soldiers now. If we try to stop them they'll kill us.'

'All right, then,' he snarled. 'That's exactly what they'll have to do, because they'll get nowt out of me while I'm living!'

SEVENTEEN

Next day I took Ben along to get the two of us registered while Dad looked after the shop. It was a frosty morning and Ben made the most of it. There were a lot of people about, most of them heading for the council offices and he dodged among them, looking for icy patches to slide on.

Most people seemed to be co-operating, in spite of the rebellious mutterings of the previous day, and I was worried as hell about Dad.

I hurried a bit, zig-zagging between the ragged figures to keep the kid in sight. I was wearing this duffel-coat with Charlie's gun in the pocket, just in case.

When we got to Market Square there was a massive queue in front of the offices. An APC was parked in the middle and three or four blokes in fallout suits walked up and down the queue with submachine-guns, keeping everybody in line.

I got hold of Ben's hand and tagged on the end of the queue. He tried to break loose. 'Gerroff!' he snarled. 'I want to see the tank.' I tightened my grip.

'It's not a tank,' I told him. 'It's an APC.'

'Well, I want to see the APC then,' he retorted. 'I'm gonna get on top of it.'

'No you're not. See that man with the gun? If he sees you by yourself he'll shoot you.'

'Will he heck!' He started trying to prize my fingers apart

with his free hand, going red in the face. I gave his arm a jerk.

'Give over Ben, will you? Dad said you'd got to stick with me.'

'Did he heck.' It was Ben's favourite word, heck. He thought it was swearing.

'Yes he did – you didn't hear him.' The queue shuffled forward a yard or so. 'We've got to wait in this queue, or else we won't get anything to eat.'

' 'Course we will!' he piped, querulously. 'What about all that stuff down the – .'

'Shaddap!' I nearly jerked him off his feet, the poor little sod. 'Ow!' He swung a kick at my shins. 'You nearly pulled my arm off, you big puff!'

'Hey!' I put on this very stern expression. 'Don't ever let me hear you use that word again. Dad'll half-kill you if he hears you.'

'Will he heck,' he snarled. 'The big puff.'

I was about to slap his head when I saw Kim. She'd just entered the square and was staring in dismay at the queue, which had lengthened since Ben and I had joined it. I waved and called to her, hoping that those behind would take us for brother and sister or something, and let her in. She spotted me and came over.

'You've taken your time,' I said, giving her a broad wink. 'Dad told you to come straight here.'

'Nuts to Dad!' She was quick on the uptake. 'I had to see someone.' She eased herself in beside me. No resentful murmurings from behind.

'Who're you?' shrilled Ben.

'Don't act the goat, Ben,' I said. 'We're not in the mood.'

'Yes, but –'

'Give over!' I crushed his knuckles.

'Who – ?'

I squeezed harder. He winced and gave in, but it was too late.

'Who is she, then?' said a voice behind us. 'Queue-jumping, are we?'

I could have murdered our Ben. I turned.

It must have been my lucky day. He was a very short, thin guy with a sharp, stubbly face under a beat-up hat. His pinched, red nose had a droplet on its tip.

'You talking to my sister, mister?' I rhymed. He eyed me nervously.

'If she's your sister, how come the kid doesn't know her?'

'Aye,' put in a woman behind him. I silenced her with a glare, then looked at the little guy.

'Listen,' I hissed. 'The nipper's fooling but I'm not. One more peep out of you and I'll chew your nose off: okay?'

He looked at me in silence for a moment. ' 'Ti'nt fair,' he muttered.

'What is?' I growled. Having no answer to this he dropped his eyes and I turned my back on him.

'You're learning,' said Kim in my ear. Her breath smelt sweet and made me tingle.

'What're you doing here, anyway?' I countered. 'I thought you'd see it as a trap or something, like my dad.' She shrugged.

'There'll be a catch in it somewhere. They're getting all our names, for one thing, but what choice is there when there's no grub?' She glanced at me sharply. 'Where is your dad, by the way?'

'At home.' I hoped she'd leave it at that.

'Guarding the stock,' she murmured. The queue shuffled forward again. I glanced around and was relieved to find nobody taking an interest in our conversation.

'Yes,' I whispered. 'His idea, not mine. Anyway, I thought you'd approve. You said if you were up at Kershaw Farm you'd hang onto what you'd got, remember?'

'It's not the same.' She snapped, out loud.

'Sssh!' I squeezed her arm. 'Somebody'll hear you. What's different about it?'

'He's one of us,' she hissed. 'He's cheating his own people. I don't know how you can defend him.'

'I'm not, but you said we've got to be as hard as they are and that's what he's being – hard.'

'Stop throwing my words back at me! And watch what you're doing.' The people in front of us had moved without my noticing. We closed the gap.

'You're illogical,' I told her. 'Like all women.'

'And you're a sexist pig!' she retorted. 'Like all men.'

'I wish you'd both shurrup,' scowled Ben. 'You sound like Mum and Dad.'

Kim caught my eye and grinned. I felt for her hand and squeezed it and we stood there like a family queueing for a movie.

EIGHTEEN

What they did was, they gave the Spacers marked cards. I mean the ones who were taken along to register. Those with no relatives or friends didn't go at all, and died when the loose grub ran out.

You can always spot a Spacer. It doesn't matter how normal you try to make them seem there's always something; eyes or hair or the way they move. Even their clothes. I can't explain but you know what I mean.

Anyway, those characters at the offices spotted them all right, and marked their cards. Nobody knew at the time, but a couple of days later when everybody trooped up to Ramsden Park with bowls and plates and spoons there were two queues.

These queues were about a quarter of a mile long and it was raining, and when some people reached the front and showed their cards they were sent to the other queue. They had to go to the back and start all over again. We had to; me and Ben. We'd joined the Spacers' queue, only nobody told us – nobody called it the Spacers' queue. They just sorted people out when they got to the front, so that it wasn't obvious what was happening.

You've probably guessed the rest. They put something in the Spacers' grub. It all looked the same: a thick, brown stew, steaming hot, served from field-kitchens under canvas by guys in fallout suits. We stood about in the rain, shoving it into our mouths, chatting. There was a bit of a party atmosphere that first time, in spite of the weather. It was great to know there'd be grub every day without our having to scavenge for it. There were soldiers dotted about with submachine-guns, looking for Goths. That was another new word; Goth. It meant anybody from outside. There were these bands of wandering people from God knows where, who'd drift in now and then looking for grub. Savages they were, with an extra-special viciousness that set them apart from the locals. It was them you had to watch out for when you went anywhere on your own. A local would usually back off if you showed him a club or something, but not a Goth. Goths were the worst, until the Purples started up.

Anyway, there were the soldiers and we felt safe. It was nice to eat without having to look around all the time like a thrush in a cattery.

It was three or four hours later that the poison started to work. I didn't see it myself but they said it was horrible. I heard some of the poor sods yelping and that was enough for me.

Next day we didn't go. The park must have been half-empty. Not only were all the Spacers missing, but a lot of other people stayed away as well. Quite a few came to us for food. It's not much fun when you don't know what you're eating.

I heard all about it afterwards though, from Kim. She said there were two queues again, and the worst thing was people's faces as they peered at their cards, comparing them; trying to decide which line was safe. If any. One or two even asked the soldiers, who thought it was no end of a laugh and gave conflicting answers; hinting first that this queue was for the chop, then that. Nevertheless people ate; hundreds and hundreds of them. Afterwards they trailed home sweating, waiting for the pains to start. It's amazing what you'll do when you're hungry.

NINETEEN

It must have been a week or so later that Ben said, 'Where's Mum?' It was dusk, and we were sitting under the awning. We'd just finished our meal. We'd never gone back to Ramsden Park after that first time, so at least Dad wasn't hoarding his stock and pinching rations as well. No soldiers had come near the shop, and I was beginning to relax.

He looked at the kid for a bit without answering, then at me. I could see he was taken aback. I mean, it was like she'd been gone about ten minutes and the kid had just missed her. I raised my eyebrows, looked at Ben and said. 'She can't be with us anymore, Ben. She wouldn't have liked it, living like this.'

He sat with his hands between his knees, his feet in heavy boots dangling. He gazed at the floor a moment, then said, 'Is she dead?'

'Yes.' I expected him to burst out crying but he didn't. He sat looking at the floor, swinging his matchstick legs so that his boot heels struck the legs of his chair again and again. Dad got up and busied himself with the dishes.

I said softly, 'D'you want to see where Dad and me put her?'

He nodded, without looking up. 'M-m. Can we go now?'

I glanced over at Dad, who nodded. 'Yes,' I said. 'We can go now if you like. It's just across the road.'

I lifted him over the counter and took him across. I hadn't been back since we'd buried her. Everything was the same, except that some weeds had grown on the mound of yellow clay. They were black; shrivelled by the frost.

Ben stared at the mound and I wondered what was going on inside his head. After a bit he said, 'Is it like being asleep, Danny?'

'Yes,' I said. 'I suppose it is.'

He pondered this. 'Does she know I'm here?'

'Well, yes, Ben, I think she knows you're here.'

'Can she hear us talk?'

'Yes.'

'How, if she's asleep?'

He had me there. I didn't answer straight away. Presently I said, 'I don't know, Ben. Nobody does. I think she hears us, that's all.'

'Well —' He bent over the mound and in a louder voice said, 'You wouldn't like it now, Mum: it's horrible.' It was the first time he'd given any sign that he was aware of our situation. I took his hand.

'Come on Ben,' I said. 'It's nearly dark.'

We were turning, when a voice behind us said, 'He who places his brother in the land is everywhere.' I turned round, and saw an old man leading a donkey on a bit of rope. I'd been so preoccupied with the kid, I hadn't heard him coming. He stopped. The donkey dropped its head and waited. 'Sam Branwell,' said the man.

I screwed up my eyes, trying to make out his features. 'Sam Branwell, the farmer?'

'Smallholder,' he corrected.

I knew his place. It was on the way to school. A little field, fenced off from the road, with some chicken-coops and a shed with goats in it. We used to call it the farm.

'What was that you said?' I asked. Ben was gazing at the donkey.

'He who places his brother in the land is everywhere,' said the old man again. 'It's a quotation.' I shrugged.

'I don't get it.'

He nodded towards the grave. 'Who's is that?'

'Our mother's,' I told him.

'And you have placed her in the land. It's happening everywhere these days and that's what the quotation means.' He didn't sound clever or anything, just sad.

'Ah.' I didn't know what else to say. He was watching us narrowly.

'Not on your own, are you?'

'What?'

'On your own. You have someone you live with; a parent or something?'

'Oh, yes.' I looked over at the shop. 'Over there: our Dad.'

I was nearly crying, if you want to know. He nodded. 'All right, then. I'd be getting back if I were you: there's Purples about.'

'Purples?' It was the first time I'd heard the word.

'Oh aye; whole pack of 'em. You stick with your dad till daylight.'

He jerked on the rope and said, 'Gaaa!' They moved away, clopping along the frosty tarmac. We watched them fade to shadow, then crossed the road.

Purples. I'd no idea what the word meant, then. If I had, we'd have moved a whole lot faster.

TWENTY

An uneventful week had lulled us into a false sense of security. I'd just got back with the water next afternoon when the soldiers came.

It wasn't like I'd pictured it: them spread out, advancing over the snow; me and Dad crouching behind the wall, blazing away and Ben safe in the cellar.

It was dusk. I handed the bucket over the counter to Dad and he carried it towards the stove, leaving the gun propped against the barricade. They must have been watching, because I was swinging myself over the counter when they came bounding from all directions.

I don't think I'd have taken them on, even if I'd had the chance. I was grabbed from behind, and they were over the counter like lightning. Ben saw them coming, grotesque in their fallout gear, and cried out, but they were onto Dad before he could turn round.

'Okay,' quacked a voice in my ear. 'Just take it nice and easy and nobody'll get hurt.' It was like something on the telly, except that the man had his arm round my throat and I was half-throttled. He slid easily over the counter, with me in one hand and the gun in the other.

Two got Dad down and sat on him, and the rest went straight to the cellar. One of them shoved Ben so hard he went sprawling and lay on the ground, howling. A truck came down the street and pulled up, and an APC lurked nearby with its engine running.

One man, a sergeant maybe, gave orders and they made a human chain, passing stuff from hand to hand up the steps while three of them scurried backwards and forwards, chucking it into the truck. There was a heck of a lot of stuff down there, but they cleaned us out in about twenty minutes while I choked under this guy's arm and Dad lay cursing on the floor.

When they were through, the man in charge said something through his mike. They hauled Dad to his feet and began dragging him towards the truck.

'Hey!' I twisted, trying to free myself. 'Leave him – he didn't make any trouble!'

The grip tightened round my throat and the guy said, 'You were warned. We'll have you along too, if there's any more of your lip!'

I struggled wildly as they bundled him over the barricade and lifted him, kicking, into the back of the truck. The soldier's arm was like a band of steel across my throat and he squeezed till I nearly blacked out. When all the others were in the truck he flung me to the ground and ran, vaulting the counter. By the time I got up, he'd scrambled into the APC.

The truck started moving, and the driver of the APC gunned his motor. I ran to the barricade, half-crazy, screaming at the top of my lungs. The APC fell in behind the truck and both vehicles lurched away down the street.

I cleared the counter and ran after them. Thin blue exhaust hung on the cold air and I ran through it, shouting God knows what in my terror.

The vehicle accelerated, pulling away from me and I suppose I was forty yards behind the APC when it blew up.

There was this terrific bang. I was lifted off my feet and flung onto my back. Bits fell all round and I rolled over, wrapping my arms round my head. The air was full of dust. I thought I heard voices, but when I tried to open my eyes the dust stung them, blinding me. I struggled to rise as tears ran down my face.

I was on my knees when the second explosion came. Debris

pattered onto the ground and I threw myself flat. The next thing I knew, there were shouts and footfalls and I staggered to my feet, dashing water from my eyes with my knuckles.

The APC was on its side, burning. Beyond it stood the truck, tilted to one side. Ragged men swarmed round it. Someone was dragging the driver down from the cab.

I stood gaping. My head reeled and I felt sick. Men were on the truck, chucking our stuff down to others who ran with it into the ruins. A man on a pile of rubble yelled, 'Make it snappy!' It was Rhodes, the PE teacher at school.

I remembered Dad and cried out, running towards the truck. I was by the APC when Rhodes yelled 'Stop there!' He came over.

'What d'you want, Lodge?' he rapped. He wore a sub-machine-gun round his neck instead of his usual whistle. He was even wearing his maroon tracksuit. He'd never liked me.

'My dad, sir!' I gasped. 'He's on the truck.' He shook his head.

'Not any more, lad. There's nothing you can do for him now.'

I stared at him, shaking my head; unable to take in what he was telling me.

'C'mon laddie, move away.' He said it as though he'd found me loitering in the cloakroom. I didn't move. It was like one of those nightmares where you're caught up in a sequence of random events and you want to run but your legs won't work. He came towards me and I saw him raise the gun and still I couldn't move.

At that moment a figure emerged from the ruins away to my right, leading a donkey. 'All right, Rhodes.' He called. 'I'll take it from here.'

TWENTY-ONE

It was Branwell, the man who'd spoken to me by Mum's grave. He came over. 'Here, take this.' He held out the halter to Rhodes. I knew from the way he said it he was mad at him. Rhodes took it and Branwell said, 'Get it loaded up. Food only. Hide the rest. And make it quick, that truck's overdue now.'

Rhodes led the animal away and the old man looked at me. 'I'm sorry about that,' he said. 'He's a damn good soldier is Rhodes, but not what you'd call sensitive. What's the trouble, anyway?'

I told him about Dad. 'Oh, God!' he cried. 'The man's a barbarian. He must've known they had a prisoner – why the devil didn't he call it off?' He gazed after the departing Rhodes. 'What did he say to you?'

I shrugged. 'He just told me, then said I was to move away.'

'Christ.' He looked shaken. After a bit he said, 'Well, you can't stay where you are. When they find out about this lot they'll be looking for someone to blame. You could move away of course, but I think it'd be best if the two of you came to us.'

'Us?' I said, unsteadily. 'Who are you? Why'd you blow up the – ?'

'Whoa!' He patted my shoulder. 'There's no time for that, lad; not now. Get your brother away from the shop. Right away. Hide in the ruins, till it's dark. Then, when things quieten down a bit, make your way to my place and we'll look after you. All right?'

'I – don't know.' Things had happened so fast there was no time to think. Dad gone. Our home and all our stuff. Bang bang bang. Pick yourself up and go on like nothing's happened. Spacers, the lot of us. I shook my head and said, 'I don't know, Mr Branwell. I don't even know if I can go on at all. Why bother, when everything's so – so ugly?'

His eyes fastened on mine. Hypnotist's eyes. 'Everything?'

'Aye!' I cried. 'Everything. Cold and hungry all the time. People getting sick and everybody trying to kill everybody else. I'm sick of it.'

Pale eyes you can't look away from. 'A little child in the midst of all this, still filled with wonder; even laughing sometimes. Ugly?'

'Don't give me that.' Pinned by that stare.

'A certain person,' he said, 'the sound of whose very name makes your insides melt – for whom you'd face a hundred Goths and win.'

'Knock it off.'

'You picture her now,' he said, relentlessly. 'Right now. You see her face and something stirs in you. Tell me.' His eyes burned into mine. 'Is the feeling you have, one of ugliness?'

'Leave her out of this, Mister,' I snapped. 'You're trying to screw me up.'

'They haven't killed that, have they?' he whispered. 'With their bombs and their hunger and their cold. They haven't killed that.'

'Leave me alone,' I said. 'Okay?'

'Very well.' He glanced away to where some men were loading stuff on the donkey. A few onlookers had gathered, and Rhodes was watching them from the top of a pile of debris. 'I'll leave you. But get that brother of yours away from the shop. And if you want to come to us, you know where I live.' He began walking away, then paused and looked back. 'She's one of us, you know,' he said softly. 'Your Kim.'

TWENTY-TWO

We put on all the clothes we had and left the shop. Charlie's gun was in my pocket, and I had a plastic carrier with our spare shoes in it.

I read this book once, about a kid in America who keeps getting expelled from schools. One time, he's walking away from this school and he looks back, trying to feel a goodbye but he feels nothing at all. Leaving the shop was like that. I mean, you'd think you'd feel something, leaving the place you were brought up in, but I didn't. I think everybody has just so much emotion in them, and no more. When it's used up, it's gone, and nothing can get to you any more. Anyway, I thought I ought to feel something and it reminded me of that book.

It was pitch dark and damn cold. I'd no plan – just to get away and maybe find somewhere warm.

The ground was covered in snow and we left prints. We walked in other people's tracks and dodged in and out of the houses in case they tried to follow. After a while we found a room with plastic over the window and some bits of carpet to sit on. We sat down with our backs to the wall and I got the gun out and watched the door, which was just visible in the gloom. I'd had to tell Ben about Dad and he was grizzling a bit.

Nothing happened for a while and I had time to think. With Dad gone and the soldiers looking for us, the future didn't look good. Food was going to be the first problem. If we showed up in Ramsden Park they'd have us. They'd taken all the loose grub they could find and it was slim pickings for anyone without a card.

Then there was warmth and shelter. We couldn't live outside, or even in unheated rooms like this one. We'd need fire, and they'd taken all the timber too – even furniture and doors. There was a fuel ration, but if we tried to collect it we'd be caught.

Protection was the other thing. Most locals had rations, but the area was crawling with desperate outsiders who'd smash your skull in for a pair of shoes or a biscuit. What chance had we, two kids with a gun we'd never fired?

It wasn't long before I realised we hadn't any choice. I didn't fancy joining anything that had Rhodes in it, but we'd have to go to Old Branwell's. Maybe the old man would keep him off my back.

I was ruminating like this when Ben said in a watery voice, 'Danny, I think I can hear a truck.'

We sat half-frozen, listening, as the truck came growling down the hill. A gear-change at the edge of town, then it was in the silent streets, its engine muffled now and then by the walls between. A silent interlude, followed by the slam of a door and the sound of a whistle. A picture in my head; a Lowry: small dark figures in the pale townscape.

Shots. A short burst and two singles. Shooting at shadows, I thought; or some innocent scapegoat. Myself, numb from the waist down like a man with a broken spine and Ben, toppling slowly sideways in his sleep – that Arctic sleep perhaps, from which there is no awakening.

Later, the motor again and Ben, unconscious at forty-five degrees.

The numbness lurking one inch below my heart: one more inch and pow! Straining my ears. Soon, the truck ascending the hill, gear by gear, like rungs on a ladder.

It took me all my time to move, and when I did I couldn't rouse Ben. He mumbled and lolled about, and even when I shook him hard he only half-opened his eyes.

I had to carry him. I staggered out of that house on frozen

legs, with the bag in one hand and the kid slung over my shoulder. I don't know how long it took me to get to Branwell's, or how I got there at all, but after what seemed a lifetime I looked up and there was the house and a light in the window.

Old Ben. He damn near killed me that night, sleeping like a lead weight on my shoulder. I wish he was sleeping there now.

TWENTY-THREE

When Branwell opened the door I nearly fell in. He caught me, propped me against the wall and lifted the kid off my shoulders.

'Good lad,' he grunted. 'I was beginning to think they'd got you. Go in.' He nodded towards a doorway from which light spilled on to the bare boards of the hallway. I went in, while he closed the outer door and carried the sleeping Ben away.

The room was a mess, but it was the best place I'd been in since the bomb. The window frame and skirting board were charred and the carpet was disintegrating. There was a table with an oil-lamp and mugs on it, a few hard chairs and a book-case with its glass front smashed. Polythene had been nailed over the windows and a wood fire flickered in the hearth.

I went over to the fire and held out my hands to the warmth. After a couple of minutes Branwell came in. 'That's it,' he said. 'You get warm. How far did you carry the child?'

I shrugged. 'Dunno. A mile, maybe. What have you done with him?'

'I've put him to bed and he's fine, so don't worry. Welcome to Masada.'

'What?' I was pressing warm hands over frozen ears and not hearing too well.

'Masada.' He smiled. 'That's what we call ourselves. It

stands for Movement to Arm Skipley Against Dictatorial Authority. Tea?'

'What?' I was still half-frozen and not at my brightest.

He smiled again. 'Would you like some tea?'

'Oh – yes,' I said. 'Yes please.'

'Take that wet coat off then, and have a seat.' He waved towards a chair. I dropped the duffel coat on the floor and sat down.

The old man wrapped a rag round his hand, lifted a blackened kettle off the fire and poured water into two mugs. Teabags popped up and he held them down with a spoon till the air bubbled out.

'Powdered milk, I'm afraid. Sugar?' I nodded. He dropped the kettle back among the flames and got a tin down from the top of the book-case. He ladled sugar into the mugs, stirred briskly and fished out the bags.

We sat with our hands wrapped round the mugs. The sodden bags lay steaming on the table. I said, 'Where's Kim?'

The old man chuckled. 'I'm sorry, old lad, she doesn't actually live here. She comes in the daytime to lend a hand. Quite a few people do.'

'Oh.' I sat gazing into the flames, wondering whether he'd deliberately mislead me. Probably not. After a bit I said, 'The people I saw, Rhodes and them. Do they live here?'

'Most of 'em.' He sipped his tea. 'Here in the house or in the paddock. We've a couple of huts in the paddock. Oh – and then there's always two or three guarding the factory.'

'Factory?'

'Yes. Across the way. Used to make toys.'

I nodded. 'I used to pass by here on my way to school. What's in there?'

He got up and put his mug on the table. 'Stores,' he said. 'And a workshop. We're making preparations.'

'For what?'

He began walking about the room with his hands in his pockets, scuffing up bits of charred carpet with his shoes.

'For a fight, unfortunately,' he sighed. 'You'd think we'd have had enough of that sort of thing, wouldn't you?'

I shrugged. 'I don't know. Are you going to fight the soldiers?'

He nodded. 'It's inevitable, I'm afraid. You see, our Commissioner and his people have learned nothing from all of this. They ought to be out, organizing food and shelter and medical help for every poor wretch they can find; trying to get life back to something resembling normality, hopeless though that might be. That was the theory, when these pathetic Commissioners were appointed. Instead, they're doing what any group does that finds itself sitting pretty in the midst of chaos. They're sitting up there at Kershaw Farm, plotting how they can hang on to their privilege. It's human nature. They'll probably try to set up a sort of feudal community, with the soldiers in their hill-fort and the peasants, that's us, toiling to feed them. And when they've got it all going, they'll start riding out armed to the teeth like knights from a castle, looking for other communities to plunder and kill. They have no reverence for life, even now. They're practically pre-Neanderthal.'

I looked at him.

'How d'you mean?'

'Well, the Neanderthals were the first people with human feelings. They took care of their sick, and buried their dead with flowers. Pre-Neanderthal people abandoned their sick and ate their dead. Nature made them brutal because only brutes could survive in the harsh world that existed then. And when, thousands of years later, we began to develop weapons of mass-destruction, nature saw what was coming and began turning us back into brutes, so that we might survive in a devastated world.'

'How were we turned into brutes?' I asked.

'We watched death and destruction on T.V. newsreels till it meant nothing to us – till it didn't shock us any more. If we'd realized in time what was happening to us, if we'd clung on to our reverence for life, then we'd never have launched those missiles. That's what I think, anyway.'

'Can we win the fight?' I asked.

He took the empty mug from my hand and put it on the table.

'We've got to,' he said. 'Because if we don't the whole thing will start again. Bigger and bigger weapons; bigger and bigger, till their power is beyond man's power to imagine and he unleashes them, or they unleash themselves.'

Pre-Neanderthal. The phrase kept repeating in my head. Pre-Neanderthal.

We sat on a while, watching the ashes settle. He didn't speak for a long time. He knew he'd given me something to think about and he was letting me do it in peace.

Presently he said, 'Come on, old lad, time you got some sleep.' He took the lamp and led me along the hallway and into a room with about ten beds in it. They were all occupied except one, and I sat down on it, half-asleep, while he helped me off with my boots. Then he went away with the lamp and I pulled the rough blankets over myself and sank at once into a dream in which I shambled like an ape-man through a desolate landscape, with a club in my hand.

TWENTY-FOUR

I woke when it was still dark to find men struggling into their clothes, grunting and cursing in the overcrowded room. I lay still, wondering whether I ought to join them. Nobody shook me or called out or anything; in fact they seemed to make every effort to be as quiet as possible, and in the end I lay with my eyes closed and the blanket up over my ear till they left the room.

When they'd gone I tried to drop off again but couldn't. My body felt warm and heavy, but my thoughts raced like an LP at seventy-eight and in the end I gave up and got out of bed.

Somebody had kicked one of my boots away, but by this time enough light showed through the dirty polythene window for me to find it.

I made my way along the passage to the room I'd sat in the night before. I expected it to be full of men but it wasn't. There was only old Branwell, lifting a big pan of water off the fire. He glanced round.

'Ah, good morning, Danny. Sleep well?' Pouring the water into a big plastic bowl.

'Yes thanks,' I said. 'It's funny, sleeping in a proper room again.'

He smiled and nodded, piling mugs and plates in the steaming bowl.

'The men didn't disturb you?'

'No.' I looked round. 'Where are they?'

'Gone.' He squirted detergent into the water, swished it to suds with a cloth and began rapidly washing mugs; twisting the cloth in them and placing them upside-down on the table.

'Where to?' I asked.

'Oh, to their various tasks – a man's got to be ready to turn his hand to anything here in Masada. A woman too, of course.'

I wondered if that was a hint and said, 'Can I wipe those for you?'

'Aye, lad, there's a cloth over there.' It had been, then. I flushed, unhooked the cloth from its nail and stood beside him, wiping hot crockery and stacking it on a dry part of the table.

'What sort of tasks?' I pursued.

The old man dumped a handful of cutlery in front of me. 'Well now, let me see. This morning most of them are burying corpses.'

'Corpses?' I glanced at him sideways.

'Corpses. The town's full of 'em. It's not so bad this time of year but if we let 'em lie till the warm weather comes – ' He shrugged. 'You know – disease. Epidemic, probably. Not a pleasant job, but it has to be done.'

'But how? I mean, there's hundreds. Thousands. It'll take years.'

He nodded. 'Without the proper equipment, yes. Of course, it's really the duty of those people at Kershaw Farm. They've got earth-moving equipment. Still, we can only do our best. A little at a time, you know.'

I nodded. 'What else happens here?'

He fished the last spoon out of the suds and grabbed a corner of my tea-towel to dry his hands. 'A few of the men are over at the factory. We've got a vehicle or two and they're doing them up, ready for when we need them. Then there are the guards over there, and a couple on the roof here. Two nurses on duty in the hospital-hut, and the rest out foraging for grub and bits of cars, stuff like that.'

'Wow!' I said. 'All this going on and nobody knows anything about it. What's the hospital hut?'

He jerked his head in the direction of the paddock. 'Hut out there. Full of people who joined us, then fell sick. Creeping doses, most of them – on their way out.'

'Creeping doses?'

'Aye. A lot of places round here are radioactive. As people wander about they accumulate radiation in their bodies till it kills 'em. Or it lowers their resistance to disease and they die of something else.'

I shivered. 'How d'you know we aren't all collecting radiation like that?'

He shrugged. 'I don't. Nobody does. It's quite possible that in a couple of years' time there'll be no such thing as a human being in England, or the world for that matter. We carry on and hope, that's all. Beans and coffee for breakfast, by the way.'

While I ate, he left the room and came back carrying Ben. The little kid knuckled his eyes and gazed about, wondering where he was. Branwell sat him on a chair and put a plate of beans in front of him. He looked across the table at me. 'What's this place, Danny?' he mumbled, still half-asleep. 'I want to go home.'

I scooped up the last of my beans. 'This is our home now, Ben,' I said with a mouth full. 'If Mr Branwell will have us, that is.' The thought gave me a sudden, euphoric lift.

The old man mussed Ben's hair. 'Of course he will, laddie; what's a house without kids, eh?'

When Ben had eaten, Branwell said, 'Now then, you fellows slept in your clothes last night and for many a night before that, by the looks of you. So, the next thing's a thorough wash and a change of clothes. Oh, yes.' He'd seen my expression. 'We're properly organized here, lad – a shower, no less, and clothing to fit all sizes. Follow me.'

I grabbed Ben's hand, and the old man led us right along the passage, through a defunct kitchen and out onto the paddock. It was the first time I'd seen it since the nukes, and it was completely different. The goat-house had gone, and three long huts now occupied most of the space. The little duck-pond was a snow-filled depression and the scraggy elders under which hens had scratched would never bear leaves again. A tarred lean-to still stood against the house wall, and it was towards this that Branwell led us.

It was pretty dark inside. We stood blinking in the doorway, till our eyes adjusted themselves and we could make out an odd structure that almost filled the lean-to. It was a sort of box perched on long wooden legs with cross-pieces nailed to the legs. It reminded me of one of those watch-towers in prisoner of war films. On the floor between the legs were two raft-like duckboards.

'What the heck's that?' I said. Branwell chuckled.

'That's the shower,' he said. 'Very proud of that, we are. Look.' There was an old saw-horse by the wall. He dragged it over and stood on it, removing one side of the box. There was a second box inside. In the space between the boxes, a safety-lantern burned. He replaced the side and got down.

'The inner box is zinc,' he said. 'It's full of water. The outer box is wood, padded with cotton-waste and polystyrene and anything else we could find. Between, on all four sides are lanterns burning spirit. The water gets quite warm overnight.'

My own spirit had just begun to soar when he added, 'Of course, that water was used up by the others. Still, the lamps'll have taken the chill off the fresh lot.'

If they had, I didn't notice. You pulled on an old lavatory-chain and it came sprinkling down like liquid ice. I gasped and dodged out from under, with Ben yelping at my heels. The old guy laughed, said we'd get used to it and handed me a hard brush and a block of gritty soap.

'Scrub each other,' he said. 'And lather your hair. I'll get rid of this lot and fetch some clean stuff.' He went out, carrying our smelly clothes and letting in an icy blast.

I won't go on about it. It was damn cold and we didn't get used to it. We managed though, and he came back with rough towels and in no time we were clean and dry and decently dressed for the first time in God knows how long. It felt so good I nearly cried.

TWENTY-FIVE

Branwell showed me how to top up the shower tank from buckets, and I spent the rest of that day chopping wood. There were all these logs, thousands of them, stacked in the angle between the lean-to and the house. Branwell gave me an axe and showed me the stump they did the chopping on.

'Split 'em good and thin,' he said. 'So they'll catch easily. We light up with paper and paper's getting scarce. This young man can help me in the house.' He went away, leading Ben by the hand.

I was so busy swinging the heavy axe that I didn't feel the cold. I was so happy I sang this old American work-song my dad had on record: Take This Hammer. It's meant to be sung by people breaking rocks but it fitted in with the chopping. The singing and swinging became automatic, and my mind was free to think.

I thought about what Branwell had said last night — that we'd have to fight eventually. I wondered why people fight. I mean, there was the Commissioner sitting up on Kershaw Farm, and here we were. We weren't bothering each other so far as I could see. Why couldn't they live the way they wanted to live, and let us live our way?

I thought about this for a bit as the pile of sticks grew beside the stump, and I saw that it was just like countries before the nukes. Some lived one way, some another. Only instead of leaving it like that they argued and threatened and built horrific weapons, and finally they launched these weapons at each other, and now we weren't living like we used to, and it's a fair bet they weren't living like they used to either. Millions of people dead, and everything worse for those who were left. Crazy.

Around midday, the door of one of the long huts opened and a woman came out wearing jeans and a sweater and carrying a tin tray. As she came by she said, 'Hey, don't you ever stop?'

I stuck my axe into the stump and grinned, wiping my forehead with the back of my hand. 'I'm keeping warm,' I said.

She smiled. 'Fine. What's your name?'

'Danny. Danny Lodge.'

'Mine's Kate. I'm a nurse. Coming for something to eat?'

'Sure. Is there something?'

She nodded. 'Oh, yes. Mr Branwell spends most of his time preparing food. There's always something for the patients, and for anybody else that's around.'

I smiled. 'It's like heaven, this place.' Kate shook her head. 'We had heaven,' she said. 'Before. We blew it up. Now we've got what we deserve. Come on.'

I walked with her into the house.

On the fire stood the great pan Branwell had heated water in that morning. Now it held a stew that bubbled and smelled good. Ben stood before it, stirring with a long wooden spoon. He looked round as we came in.

'Look,' he crowed. 'I made it.' He scooped a dollop and let it fall back in the pan. Kate raised her eyebrows and nodded. 'Looks good to me – how old are you?'

He glowed. 'Seven.'

'Seven?' cried Kate. 'My goodness. I couldn't cook like that when I was seven. What's your name?'

'Ben.'

'Well, Ben, I hope you're going to let me taste your stew?'

'Yes.' Pink with pleasure. The nurse looked at me.

'Did he come in with you?' I nodded.

'He's my brother. Our parents are dead.'

'Ah-ha. Well, you'll be all right here.'

Branwell came in. We served ourselves and sat round the table, Kate and I smacking our lips for Ben's benefit. Afterwards, Kate loaded her tray with plates of stew. I got up.

'Here, let me take it for you.'

'All right,' she smiled. 'Thanks.'

I lifted the tray and she led me down the passage and outside. A wind had got up, with snow flurries in it. Kate opened the hut door and turned, holding out her hands for the tray. 'I'll bring it in,' I said.

'No.' The smile left her face. 'No, you won't.'

'Why not?'

She regarded me gravely. 'Have you seen a man with a creeping dose?' I shook my head. 'I've seen 'em dead though, and burned. Can't be worse than that.'

'Can't it?' Her eyes flashed, then became sad. 'One of these days I'll show you, Danny, but not today. Give me the food before it freezes in this wind.'

I handed it to her and she turned with it into the doorway. I glimpsed another woman by the door, then it swung to. I shrugged and returned to my axe.

The wind went on rising and the snowflakes whirled round me but I chopped steadily, singing to myself, till it began to get dark. As the dusk deepened, people started coming in in twos and threes. Some came empty-handed, others had bundles or buckets or bulging pockets. The driven snow whitened their clothes and they moved with their heads down and their hands in their pockets. When they heard the axe, they'd peer in my direction, and one or two came to the corner for a closer look. I'd decided to finish this one log and pack it in when I noticed Rhodes. He was standing by the corner of the house, watching me. He came over.

'It's snowing, Lodge,' he said.

I nodded and swung the axe. 'I know.' I nearly said sir. Why should he get sir when nobody else did?

'There's a house behind you, lad.' Sarcasm was his thing. Some of the boys at school used to think he was funny, but I'd always disliked him for it. 'It doesn't snow in houses,' he continued. 'Come on in and see.'

'I'm finishing this log.'

He sniggered. 'I won't wait then; looks like you're as slow as you ever were.'

Anger flared in me. 'Nobody asked you to wait.'

'What?' he said, sharply. I twisted the axe in the split log and looked sideways at him.

'I said, nobody asked you to wait.'

'Now you listen.' He took a step towards me. 'I don't know why Branwell brought you here, but since he has you'd better know where you stand.' He thrust his face at me. 'I don't like you, Lodge – never did. You're useless at games and not so hot at anything else.

'I'm second in command around here, which means that if anything happens to that old man, I take over.' He straightened. 'So you'd better watch yourself, lad. Some might forget how you sat on all that stuff but I shan't. A bit of respect and a lot of hard work; that's what I'll be looking for from you, lad – and if I don't get it you'll be out of here so fast your feet won't touch.'

He spun on his heel and stalked off. I gazed after him, then raised the axe and sent it whistling through the log. If I'd known then what Rhodes was to become, I'd have put it through his head.

TWENTY-SIX

That night was easily the best I'd known since the Bomb. The place was full of people. Men and women, padded out in layers of old clothes, talking. There were only about four chairs, so everybody sat on the floor. You couldn't move. There was more of the stew, but plates were short, and we ate in relays. People kept coming in all the time. Every time someone came in, somebody else would shout something to them, and everybody would laugh. One man had a mouth-organ. Tea came round, and we took gulps and passed the mugs along as guys began singing. Old Branwell fussed about over his pots and pans, seeing that everybody got fed. Ben dodged about, collecting empty mugs and passing them to the old man for refills. It was freezing outside, but in that room it was warm and close and steamy. I guess it smelled a bit, but nobody minded that. We were together, and it felt like nothing terrible had happened at all.

I was joining in this song I knew, when I looked towards the door and there was Kim. She had a big can in her hand and was talking to a man. I felt a stab of jealousy and stood up. As soon as she saw me, she beamed and smiled and I knew it was all right. I began threading my way towards her through the singers.

What she'd done was, she'd gone round collecting petrol out of wrecks. There were old cars everywhere. Lorries and buses too, but it wasn't easy to find any with their tanks intact. Most of them had blown up with the heat when the nukes went off, but here and there you could still find one that hadn't. They had bodies inside, some of them, but Kim didn't care. It was her way of helping Masada.

She'd been asking the man where he wanted the petrol. Last time she'd brought some, it had been stashed in the lean-to where the shower was, but it wasn't there now. He'd told her there was too much to keep it there now. It had to go over to the factory. She let me carry it over for her. We talked, walking with our heads down against the driven snow.

'When did you get here?' she wanted to know. I told her the whole story. Dad and that. She said she was sorry, which can't have been true really, but it's one of those things people say.

Then I said, 'Why don't you move in? I mean, if you want to help, why not come and live here like all the others?'

She shrugged. 'I dunno. There's Maureen, my sister, and Mike. We manage all right at the house. I don't think they'd want to come here really. They haven't been married long. They like to be together, you know – without a lot of others around.'

I laughed, flushing and said, 'I don't blame Mike, anyway. Not if Maureen looks anything like you.' I hadn't meant to say anything like that, but it felt like an opportunity, if you know what I mean. To let her know how I felt. Not that she didn't know already, surely. Anyway, I'd said it now. I looked sideways to see how she took it.

She was quiet for a minute. We went in the factory gate. She was about to say something when a voice rapped out 'Halt!' We pulled up sharp. A figure loomed out of the murk. A muffled-up woman with a submachine-gun. She peered at us. 'Who are you?'

'Kim Tyson,' said Kim. 'With petrol for the store. I help sometimes.' The woman nodded.

'I recognize you now, Who's this?' Pointing with the gun.

'Danny Lodge,' said Kim. 'He lives here.' The woman came closer and studied my face.

'All right,' she said. 'I'll know you in future. Petrol goes over there, green door in the corner. Don't hang about.'

We put the can in the store. There were hundreds of cans, all shapes and sizes, and some bottles. The woman watched us from the gate. We walked back to her, leaving prints. She nodded as we passed, her fringe flecked with snow. She must have been frozen.

As we neared the house I said, 'You were going to say something back there. Before the sentry stopped us.' I stopped walking; holding her back by the sleeve. She looked at the ground.

'Yes,' she murmured. 'I was going to say I like you too, Danny. A lot. If things were as they used to be, I'd be your girl. I'll be your girl now, if you like, only I don't think we ought to do anything about it. Not now. Not till we see how things work out. D'you know what I mean?'

I nodded. My heart was going like mad and I wanted to take her in my arms and never let go. When I tried to, she pulled away.

'No.' She stood a little way off, straightening her coat. 'That's what I mean, Danny. It's easy to get carried away. We don't know what's going to happen: what sort of world it's going to be. We don't even know if we'll be here a month from now. Let's just wait and see how it goes. Okay?'

I inhaled slowly; drawing in sharp, cold air. 'Okay.' I moved closer and held out my hands to her.

She took them, squeezing briefly. 'I've got to go now. It'll be all right, Danny. You'll see.' She pulled me suddenly to her. Her lips brushed mine and then she was gone; hurrying away into the whirling flakes, leaving the scent of her hair in my nostrils.

I went into the house. Everybody was back by now, and the place was packed. Ben had disappeared, I guessed Branwell had packed him off to bed. It was hot and smoky and filled with raucous singing. I found a space on the floor and squeezed into it, sitting with my arms wrapped round my knees. I felt happy. Really happy for the first time since the nukes. It was partly Kim, and partly the atmosphere in that tatty, smoke-filled room. It lasted till late, when a lot of people had s"pped away to their beds and the guy with the mouth-organ started a sad sounding tune. Suddenly then, everybody went quiet, except for about three people around the musician. They began singing this song, all about our situation. I can't remember it now. Only the last bit, a couple of lines that brought tears to my eyes and echoed in my skull all night when I went to bed:

> '. . .echoes will answer the names they will call,
>   and ashes will smother the tears as they fall.'

That's how it was. Even when we thought we were happy, we were thinking of what we had lost.

TWENTY-SEVEN

It wasn't till the next morning that I discovered the reason for the sing-song. It had been Christmas Eve. At least Branwell, who tried to keep track of time, said it was. He had this little toy fire-engine he'd got from somewhere, and he gave it to Ben when he came in to breakfast. I'd thought it was just what they did there at night – the sing-song I mean. When the others had gone out I said, 'I didn't know it was Christmas. They didn't sing carols or anything.'

Branwell dumped some dishes in hot water. 'No,' he said. 'Funny, that. Someone started one; must have been while you were over at the factory. A few joined in, then it sort of fizzled out. They stopped singing, one by one. Perhaps it was too sad, y'know?'

I knew. I still heard the end of that other song in my head. Anyway, apart from the sing-song and Ben's fire-engine, Christmas was an ordinary time for us. It was special for everybody else in Skipley though.

What happened was, the loud-speaker came round again, telling everybody to stand by for a special instruction. Some wag started a rumour that a full Christmas Dinner was to be served in Ramsden Park: he must have known what day it was, too. Some of the guys in Masada were in town, and they heard the whole thing. It went like this.

Starting that day, every able-bodied adult had to report to

Kershaw Farm each morning for work. Anybody who didn't work, didn't eat. The Local Commissioner had worked out a plan for the building of 'dwellings' and the planting of crops. It was all to do with National Recovery. The people were to abandon Skipley as soon as they had built themselves dwellings on the hillside below the Farm. Then a fence would be erected round these dwellings, for the protection of those within, and soldiers would patrol this fence at all times. This development, said the announcement, would mark the beginning of a return to normal life for the people of Skipley.

That evening, when everybody had returned to the house, old Branwell called us together. The people who had heard the special instruction had told him all about it. He stood looking down at us as we sat on the floor. His face was grim.

'Well, my friends,' he began. 'The thing we have feared from the first is beginning to happen.' He outlined the content of the special instruction, then went on, 'We all know what that means. It means that our exalted Commissioner, whoever he is, has decided to start building his little feudal village. Kershaw Farm will be the Manor House, or castle, and the Commissioner will be the Lord. The soldiers, and everybody else up there, will be the knights, squires, reeves and so forth. They will sit in the Manor, living off the labour of the serfs. The serfs will be the people of Skipley. They'll toil all year, growing food, and then the Lord and his gang will pinch most of it and leave them the scraps. And there's nothing the people can do about it, because they're dependent on Kershaw Farm for their grub. That's why we banded together to form Masada: we're *not* dependent on Kershaw Farm and they'll not make serfs out of us!'

There was some cheering when he said this, but he stopped it pretty quick. 'No!' he cried. 'This is not a time to be cheering. This is a time to beware. They know we're here, those people up at the Farm. They've a fair idea we've been knocking off the odd truck now and again. They know we're a threat to their plans, and they'll stop at nothing to break us up. From now on, we must be even more alert than we've been so far. We must strengthen the guard on this house, and on the factory. We must work faster on the vehicles we are mending, and on the other equipment too. We always knew we'd have to fight some day, and that day is drawing near. I will be consulting this evening with Mr Rhodes and our various experts, and detailed instructions will be issued later tonight. Meanwhile, let us all go about our usual tasks, and remain calm.'

One of the detailed instructions was that I was to start taking my turn on sentry duty with someone else, every third night. I was glad to be of some use. I'd managed to hide Charlie's pistol up till now, but I turned it in to old Branwell and he was over the moon. 'Gold, my boy.' he said. 'Pure gold. We need every weapon we can lay hands on.'

It was tense for a few days, like guarding the shop. We expected them to come any minute, but they didn't. I reckon they were too busy supervising the work that had started on the hillside above the town. Long huts were going up, sprouting like magic from the snow. Our people watched from a distance all the time. Within a couple of weeks it was like a village up there, or a camp. We nick-named it Butlin's. 'What's happening up at Butlin's?' But as the winter wore on, and news started trickling in of what was happening to the people, we gave it another name. Belsen.

TWENTY-EIGHT

It was about a month before the defectors started coming in. The huts were finished by that time, and most of the people were living up there on the hillside. Skipley was deserted, except for a few individuals and families like Kim's, reluctant to attach themselves to any group. They brought stuff in to us, and we fed them.

We'd erected a barrier across the road between the house and the factory. I was on guard at this barrier one morning when I spotted two miserable-looking men coming along the road. At first I took them for people from the town, coming in to eat. They had nothing with them, but then it wasn't always possible to find anything with which to pay for a meal, and old Branwell always fed anyone who turned up – even Goths, as long as they behaved themselves. I released the safety-catch on the pistol and stood watching them come in.

It was sleeting, a blustery, early-February morning; and they held their rags about them as they came, glancing over their shoulders from time to time as though in fear of pursuit. As they approached, I was struck by the thinness of their features and their stick-like wrists and ankles. We were none of us fat by this time, but these men looked like walking skeletons. They stopped five yards from the barrier and one of them spoke; eyeing my pistol as he did so.

'We're from up there.' He jerked his head in the direction of the camp, invisible beyond the shoulder of the hill. 'We've broken out. We want to join you.'

I looked at them. The one who had spoken was bad enough, but the other guy was obviously dying. Most of his hair had gone, he was bleeding from the gums and great, purple blotches stained his skin. I'd seen enough radiation-sickness by this time to recognize a creeping dose, and I reckoned he'd be dead in a week. Sooner, if he was lucky.

'All right,' I said. 'I'll get somebody to take you to Mr Branwell. He'll tell you if you can stay or not.' I saw desperation in their eyes and added, 'He'll feed you and let you rest, whether or not.'

I called out to my fellow sentry, dozing in the factory gatehouse, and he led the two skeletons away. I didn't know it then, but they were to be the first of many. From them, and others like them, we got to know what was going on up by Kershaw Farm.

As soon as the huts were built, the people had been compelled to move into them. They were not allowed to bring with them any sick or elderly relatives. If they had such relatives, they were free to return to the ruins of Skipley and care for them there, but in that case there would be no more rations for them. By that time their spirit was thoroughly broken, and few chose to leave.

They were to make a farm. Working with their bare hands mostly, they had first to scrape off and carry away the top two inches of soil. This was because the top two inches were full of radioactive particles, and nothing would grow in them. It was January. The ground was usually hard with frost, and tools; even hand-tools, were scarce. Nevertheless, driven by soldiers who used their rifle-butts freely, the toilers were forced to take off this irradiated soil and wheel it away in barrows to a dumping-ground well away from the camp. The hours of work were long and the food inadequate.

When somebody fell ill, or became too exhausted to work, he was led away to the 'hospital', from which he never returned. Injections at this hospital were of lead, administered through a revolver. People worked till they died, rather than go there. It was not surprising, then, that we started getting escapees coming to us for shelter.

It led to trouble inside Masada, though. A lot of the defectors were sick, and Rhodes and some others thought we shouldn't take them. They were a drain on our resources, and contributed nothing to our cause.

Branwell argued that if we started turning people away to die, we were as bad as those in charge up at Kershaw Farm. Most of us were on his side, and so Rhodes and his lot retreated muttering. Things weren't quite the same afterwards. There wasn't the feeling that we were all in together: there were enemies inside, as well as out.

We were forced to change our tactics, too. Before, we'd sat and waited to see what the other side would do, while preparing for eventual conflict. Now, a sense of urgency prevailed. The enemy was even now killing the people of Skipley, and I think it was in Branwell's mind to attempt a rescue, as soon as we had the necessary equipment. Instead of knocking off the occasional truck, he had us out nearly every night; looking for soldiers with vehicles or stuff we might pinch. It all suited Rhodes, of course. He was a bastard, but even I had to admit he could organize an ambush that was a work of art. We struck, and fled, and struck again. The Commissioner's response was to send heavier and heavier escorts with his trucks, but we attacked them anyway, and while we suffered some casualties, our stock of equipment and weapons grew. I wasn't always with the attackers, of course – Branwell operated a sort of roster – but I saw quite a bit of action one way and another, and I'd seen enough horror by now for it not to bother me. What did bother me was that the women insisted on taking their turn on the ambush parties, and Kim was one of them. She was still living in the ruins, but now she came at night as well as during the day, and got herself put on the list.

I sweated every time she went out, but in the event it was I who came unstuck.

TWENTY-NINE

It was a simple trap, and we fell into it. Rhodes should have suspected something, but maybe he was having an off day or something. Anyway, this is how it happened.

There were six of us. Rhodes and the others had sub-machine-guns, and I had my pistol. It was late, around one or two a.m. I guess. We were in the bushes beside the Skipley Branford road. We knew some trucks had gone out that morning in the Branford direction, with an APC and a couple of motor-bikes. We had only to wait, and eventually they'd pass this way.

Rhodes had this trick with plastic bowls. He had some bowls in grey plastic, and when he wanted to stop a vehicle, he'd plant one of these bowls upside-down in the middle of the road. If it was a wide road he'd put three or four in a line. The first vehicle was usually an APC, and when the driver spotted the bowls he'd stop. They were all jumpy, because of the number of ambushes we'd pulled, and unless you were very close the bowls looked like some sort of landmine. Anyway, the APC nearly always stopped, and we'd lie low till the driver or some crew member got out to take a closer look. Then we'd lob a grenade or a bottle of petrol into the APC and go for the truck pulled up behind. It hardly ever failed, except if a driver took his vehicle round the bowls by driving off the road, and all the others followed.

What happened this time was, a truck came by itself, and when the driver saw the bowl in his headlight, he pulled up. Like I said, we should have known. Trucks just didn't go round alone anymore.

Anyway we didn't, and when the driver got out and started walking up the road, Rhodes yelled 'Go!' We crashed through onto the road, firing. The driver flung himself into the verge, and then all hell broke loose. There was a roar of motors and two APCs came round the bend, shooting. They had spotlights on them. Blinded, we milled about in the roadway, and then another APC came from the other side. We were caught in the middle. Rhodes was yelling 'Back! Into the trees!' but I couldn't see, and then something hit me and I fell. There was this terrific noise all round and blinding light. I thought I'd been shot. I lay with my eyes screwed tight, waiting to die. All I could think about was Ben. Then I passed out.

When I came to I was lying on the floor in a room somewhere, with a guy looking down at me. It was Booth. Alec Booth. Before the nukes he was the worst bully in school. It took me back, lying there with him looking down at me. It made the whole thing seem unreal somehow.

'Hello, Lodge,' he sneered. 'Been by-byes, have we? Playing at soldiers, were we?'

It was the same old Booth. Usually he'd say, 'What're you staring at,' or 'What's that you said?' and no matter how you replied, it was the wrong answer and then he'd beat you up. This time I remained silent, but that wasn't right either and he kicked me in the side with his boot.

'I said, "Playing at soldiers, were we?" ' he repeated, in a dangerously soft voice. It dawned on me that I was a sort of prisoner of war, and that Booth was interrogating me. Terror washed over me when I remembered into whose hands I had fallen, because I realized quite suddenly that I was going to die. I wondered for an instant why they hadn't killed me already, back there on the road, and then I knew why. They wanted something from me. Some information.

I'd read stories about spies in enemy hands, holding out against the most dreadful tortures. Saying nothing. I'd fantasized about being in a similar position myself: remaining silent while they pulled out my toenails and pushed hot needles into my flesh. My fantasies always ended with my being rescued; battered, emaciated, but silent to the end; flying home a hero to convalesce at length with a chestful of medals while our armies, their secrets unrevealed, swept on to total victory. I knew, now that I was faced with the reality, that I wouldn't last five minutes.

Booth was speaking again in his quiet, dangerous voice, something about Masada. For some reason, I was remembering a film I saw once, about this prisoner of war who got himself sent home by pretending to be barmy. It was a true story from the Second World War. It had nothing to do with my situation but I was the proverbial drowning man, drowning in his own terror, and I clutched at it like a straw.

A Spacer. I'd pretend to be a Spacer. Spacers don't know anything. There'd be no point torturing a Spacer for information. It never occurred to me at the time that they'd simply shoot me. All I was bothered about then was how to avoid being tortured. I turned blank eyes up to my tormentor.

He kicked me again, twice, in the same place. I doubled up and held my side, groaning; praying that he'd ask me something before the next kick, so that I might demonstrate my madness.

He bent down with an oath, grabbed me by the collar and jerked me onto my back. I stared up through tear-filled eyes, letting my jaw go slack.

'Masada,' he snapped. 'What's Masada, Lodge? What're you trying to do, eh?'

I gazed vacuously up into his coarse, vicious features. If the Commissioner had chosen Booth to be his chief interrogator, he couldn't have picked a better man. He drew back his foot.

I forced myself not to flinch away and, grinning stupidly at the naked lightbulb, said, 'I've been busy.'

'Busy?' He squatted, seized a fistful of my coat and hauled me up till I was half sitting. 'Doing what, sunshine? That's what I want to know.'

'I've had to burn all my biscuits because of them mice,' I told him. 'I had them in a tin right at the back of the cupboard but when I went to get one they tasted funny and I had to burn them all.' I let my head loll to one side and began to cry. 'Nothing goes right for me, mister. Nothing. I used to keep the butter on the windowsill till the sun made it melt. You wouldn't think it, would you? You can't even leave your butter on the window-sill. I'm fed up.'

Booth's expression shifted and he muttered something under his breath. He let go my coat and I let my head hit the floor. He straightened up with an exclamation of disgust. 'Spacer!' He walked away, turned suddenly and shouted. 'Effin' Spacer! What were you doing on that road, eh?'

I giggled wetly. 'I'm asleep, and they put the light on and start making a noise. Nothing goes right for me, mister. Nothing.'

'Spacer.' He came and looked down at me again. 'You always were a snivelling little creep, Lodge, and now you're a Spacer, aren't you? A gawping Spacer who doesn't know if he's on this earth or fuller's.' His hands twitched as though longing to strangle somebody and his face was tight with frustration. He watched me silently for a moment, then said, 'You know what we do to Spacers, Lodge, don't you?'

I'd been so relieved that my ruse seemed to be working that I hadn't thought what they'd do if they fell for it. Now it hit me like a sledgehammer, and I almost gave myself away. I almost cried out 'No!' or something like that, but I was trapped now in my own deception. If I showed fear – if I even indicated that I understood, then the interrogation would recommence. Weak with terror, I forced myself to smile and say, 'Nothing goes right, mister. Nothing.'

Without warning he bent, grabbed me by the collar with both hands and hauled me onto my feet. My side hurt where he'd kicked me and my legs were rubbery. I staggered when he let go, so he seized my arm and snarled. 'Come on. Let's clear it with the boss and get it over!' He began hustling me across the room. I could scarcely stand and wanted to vomit. He wrenched open a door with his free hand and we went along a dim corridor with a stone floor. We passed a window. I glanced through a saw a muddy yard and what looked like a barn, and I knew we were at Kershaw Farm.

We turned a couple of corners and passed some doors, till we came to one with 'Commissioner' on it in white paint. Booth shoved me up against the wall and knocked. A voice said, 'Enter.' I remember wondering why the guy didn't just say come in like everybody else.

He pushed me in first and there was Finch, sitting behind a green metal desk. Councillor Finch, the coal-merchant who was always getting his picture in the Times. The Skipley Times, not the big one. He came to our school once, talked about how the town was run. I don't know who I'd expected to see when Booth shoved me in there, but it certainly wasn't Councillor Finch. It was as much as I could do to keep from showing recognition. He hunched forward with his elbows on the desk, looking into my face.

'Ah!' he said. 'The prisoner. A child, I see. What has he to tell us, Colonel?'

'Col –?' I had begun to exclaim, glancing at Booth over my shoulder, before I could check myself. Finch's brows went up. 'Yes? What were you about to say?'

Colonel Booth. It was fortunate for me that, even in this extremity, the title struck me as ludicrous. I laughed, more loudly than the joke merited; putting it on. Booth, standing by my shoulder, said, 'He doesn't know anything, sir. He's a Spacer.'

Finch's gaze flicked from my face to Booth's and his expression hardened. 'I gave instructions that one of those swine from Messina, or whatever it's called, was to be captured alive. Why do you bring me this – thing?' He indicated me with a disdainful flap of his pudgy hand.

'Masada, sir,' said Booth. 'He was with them, sir. I mean, he was on the road when we closed in. We weren't to know he wasn't one of them, sir.'

'Weren't to know!' spat Finch, disgustedly. He eyed me again. 'How d'you know he's a Spacer?'

My heart lurched. Booth said, 'I knew him, sir, before. At

school. He was always soft, sir; not the sort to join guerilla movements. He's a Spacer all right, sir.'

'Then what the devil was he doing on that road?'

Booth shrugged. 'Sleeping I expect, sir – in the bushes. The shooting disturbed him and he ran right into the middle of it. I'm sorry, sir.'

'Bit late for that.' Finch seemed suddenly to lose interest. He reached for some papers, riffled through them and, after a moment, glanced up. 'Well, Colonel. What're you waiting for?'

'Sir?'

Finch flapped his hand in exasperation. 'Get him out of here, Booth. Take him out and shoot him. And have a genuine member of Masada here this time tomorrow. That's all.'

Fear all but overwhelmed me. I would certainly have fallen, but Booth grabbed my arm and led me out of the room. I was too shocked to resist. We went along a whitewashed passage and out into the yard. By the outside door a guy in a radiation suit stood with a submachine-gun. Booth said something to him and he handed over the gun. As we walked across the mud I kept looking at it in horrid fascination as it bounced on Booth's shoulder; the instrument of my death. I wondered where he'd do it.

We walked round the barn, and there before me was the camp we called Belsen – rows of wooden huts stretching away down the slope. Between the camp and the farm was a high barbed-wire fence with a gate in it. The gate was guarded by two men and a dog. Outside the camp, away to our left, lay the farm they were making; a great patch of raw earth with figures scattered across it, stooping, lifting, pushing barrows, while fallout-suited soldiers looked on.

We turned right, leaving the yard through a double fence. Between the fences, the ground had been cleared and flattened, and lamps strung like a necklace on cable along its length. Every forty or fifty yards there was an elevated watch-tower, like a prison-camp in a movie. All of this I saw in a kind of stupor as I walked towards my death. Thoughts chased one-another at random across my skull. Where do they get power for the lamps? What'll become of Ben? Where's he going to kill me? Oh, Kim.

We walked down the slope, with the single fence of the camp on our left. The ruins of Skipley lay spread out before us. Everything was crystal clear in my brain. I remembered reading somewhere that the imminence of death concentrates the mind. It does, too. We stopped by the bottom corner of the fence. He shoved me up against one of the posts and I thought, 'This is it.' There was no panic, no frenzy. Too late for that, I suppose. He'd back off a few paces, raise the gun, and then . . . Better than torture. Better than a creeping dose. Better than betraying my friends.

I became aware that my executioner was speaking, and focussed my attention on his words. Knowing him, I expected taunts, a little gloating to prolong the agony. What he said was, 'You're a right prannock, aren't you, Lodge? I've seen more Spacers than you've had hot dinners, and if you're a Spacer I'll eat spiders. Fooled the boss, though. Didn't know you had it in you. Still, you can thank your luckies it was me that got you. Anyone else and you'd be dead, right?' He rammed the muzzle of the gun hard into my gut. As I doubled up he stepped back, and as I fell he kicked me in the face.

I collapsed onto my side. I would have stayed there but he bent, grabbed my shirt and hauled me upright. I was choking on blood. My nose bubbled when I breathed and there was a blinding pain behind my eyes.

'That's so you'll remember to tell your mates – stay away from Kershaw. Even Spacers don't forget a boot in the kisser.' He pointed the gun upwards and fired a short burst. He waited a few seconds, then squeezed off a single shot. Then he took my arm and began steering me towards the road. I was too busy trying to keep the blood and snot out of my mouth to take much notice. The next thing I knew he said something I didn't catch and left me there on the tarmac.

It's not true what they say, that there's some good in all of us. Not after nukes, it isn't. Still, there must have been something in old Booth. It goes to show you never can tell.

THIRTY

I don't know how long it would have been before we considered ourselves ready to have a go at them. Quite a while, probably. We were trying to get hold of some proper vehicles, something to match their APCs, but we never did. What happened was, they poisoned the well.

Branwell blamed himself afterwards, but I reckon he'd done all he could. He'd realized some time before that the well was the key to our survival outside the DC's camp. It had the only clean water for miles around, except for the well at Kershaw Farm. He'd put a day and night guard on it: two guys with Submachine-guns, relieved every four hours. Whenever the guard changed, the guys who'd finished their spell carried water back to the house. They were the only people allowed to take water from the well, except for the odd groups I mentioned before; those still living in the ruins.

Anyway, they came in the middle of the night, without vehicles. Just a commando-squad, I suppose, moving silently and carrying poison. When the relief went out at six they found the guards with their throats cut and some empty containers that had had weedkiller in them, paraquat or something. Old Branwell knew all about weedkillers. He reckoned it'd be weeks at least before the water would clear itself, if it ever did. He realized there was only one chance for us now, we had to take Kershaw Farm.

Branwell asked to see me. I didn't feel like going. I'd been laid up for two days, ever since I'd got back from my encounter with Booth. My jaw was one big bruise and Kate, the nurse, reckoned I had a couple of cracked ribs. I was all strapped up and feeling sorry for myself, even though everybody said I was lucky they hadn't shot me. I got off my bed and went through to the big room.

Branwell was there, with Rhodes and some others. They had this map on the table, an Ordnance Survey map of Skipley and the surrounding area. I joined them and Rhodes gave me a dirty look.

Branwell said, 'Now then, Danny: here's where your recent unpleasant experience can be turned to good use. We need to know a bit about the layout up at the Farm.' He tapped the map where Kershaw Farm was shown, a cluster of minute buildings on the edge of the moor. I bent over it, wincing from the pain in my ribs.

'Well,' I began, feeling daft. They were all watching me as though I was Field Marshal Montgomery or something. I tried to recall everything I'd seen during that unreal walk with Booth that might have ended in my death. 'All this is surrounded by a double fence, with lights over it.' I circled the Farm with my finger.

Rhodes made an impatient noise. 'We know that,' he snorted. 'We can see that from the outside.'

Branwell gave him a sharp look and said, 'What about the buildings themselves, Danny? Can you tell us which buildings are used for what?'

'Hm.' I chewed my swollen lip, trying to remember. 'The house itself has offices in it. Rooms that have been made into offices. One is the Commissioner's office. Then there was one that said "Food Officer" on it, and another to do with health. There's a kitchen, and I think I heard kids upstairs somewhere.' I knew I wasn't doing too well. I could feel Rhodes' sarcastic eyes on me and I flushed.

'It's all right, Danny,' said Branwell. 'Just take your time and try to remember. You were under a great strain at the time. We all appreciate that. What about the soldiers?'

I frowned. 'There were some huts. Here, I think. They're not on the map.' I pointed to an empty bit among the buildings. 'They were long, and new-looking, and there were a few men in radiation-gear hanging about outside them.'

Branwell nodded. 'That sounds about right. Did you notice any vehicles?'

'Yes.' I recalled this part vividly, and pointed to an area between the farmhouse and where the camp now was. 'Here. There were some APCs, some trucks and some cars, all parked together on a concrete pad. 'A motorbike, too.'

'Did you notice any well?' put in Rhodes. I nodded. 'It's in the yard. Right by the house.' I bent over the map. 'Here.'

'Aha!' Branwell, who had been scrutinising the map closely, straightened up. He glanced at the men and women round the table. 'Do any of you notice anything?' He was smiling. They looked at him blankly. All except Rhodes, who smiled faintly and nodded, looking at the others with his mocking eyes. Branwell said, 'Tell them, Keith.' Keith. I'd often wondered what the K was for.

Rhodes smirked, enjoying his moment. 'Everything that matters,' he said, 'Is concentrated at one end of the yard, the eastern end. And the soldiers are at the other. Look.' He pointed. 'The house, the well and the vehicle-park; all here at the east end of the yard. If we take the east end, we've cut the soldiers off from their vehicles and their orders, we've got the Commissioner and we control the water supply. They've no option but to surrender!'

Everybody started talking at once. My ribs were killing me. Old Branwell asked me a couple more things, then told me I could go.

I wandered back to the room I shared with nine other men. They were all out and I lay on the bed, thinking about the coming fight and whether I'd still be alive at the end of it. If it hadn't been for Ben, sleeping upstairs, and Kim out there somewhere, I don't think I'd have cared much either way.

THIRTY-ONE

Thirst is a terrible thing. I'd never thought much about it before. Branwell rationed what little water we had at the rate of a cupful a day for everybody. By everybody, I mean all the members of Masada, and anybody else who showed up.

Rhodes went mad. 'Don't dole it out to all and sundry!' he raved. 'Save it for us. We've got to keep our strength up.' Branwell let him rant, and carried on as before. Most of us were on his side. When the water in the buckets ran out, we started on the shower-tank.

It was April, and warm for the time of year. On the second day, some people drank from the well and died. We had to put a guard on it again. People started drinking from puddles, sucking in radioactive muck that would kill them slowly. A few went and gave themselves up at the camp.

We worked flat out. We had a Land-Rover and three cars. We fitted armour-plating over the windscreens with eye-slots, and mounted a heavy machine-gun on the Rover, and a spotlight too. There were two motor-bikes; we made rough side-cars from them out of scrap and put machine-guns on them as well. There was a rocket-launcher with one rocket. We fitted that to one of the cars. Apart from that, we had about twenty automatic rifles and submachine-guns. The rest of us would have to make do with shotguns, pistols and a hotch-potch of home-made weapons. There was even a crossbow.

It was on the fourth day that Ben disappeared. I'd been across at the factory all day, helping get the vehicles ready. It was starting to get dark when Branwell came running. 'Danny!' he called from the loading-bay door. 'Danny, come quick! The little lad's gone!'

It was the thirst. What happened was, the old man gave everybody their cup of water after breakfast each day, but he kept Ben's on a high shelf so he wouldn't drink it all at once. That morning, Ben had complained, and Branwell had tried to explain that it was for his own good. Ben had sulked and, at some point during the day, left the house. Branwell hadn't noticed his absence, being too busy planning the assault on the Farm, until, at dusk, he realized the kid hadn't asked for any of his water.

I was frantic. The old man organized search-parties with flash-lights and whistles. Kim came. She spoke to me, telling me not to worry, but I was so distraught I hardly knew she was there. I was thinking of all the disasters that might befall a little boy out there in the dark. When the parties started leaving I didn't go with them, I set out alone, having begged Branwell to let me take my pistol.

As night fell, it grew cold. I'd stripped off most of my padding during the morning and now had on only shirt and trousers. My teeth chattered as I went, and I couldn't tell how much of it was cold, and how much fear.

I went right through Skipley. Except for the occasional shouts of the searchers, the ruined town was still. I moved through the rubble-strewn streets at a half-run, calling Ben's name, and soon the search-parties were far behind me. I didn't know where I was going. I was in too much of a state to work to a plan. It must have been some sort of instinct that took me in the right direction while everybody else floundered about miles away. Either that, or sheer coincidence.

I was on this long road, Canal Road, though there was no canal now. I was loping along, breathing hard, the pistol in my hand. The buildings thinned. There was a long stretch of rough grassland, waste land really, where houses had been cleared a long time ago. It was one of those places where travelling-people used to park their caravans and tether their shaggy ponies, where other folk came at night to dump their old mattresses and three-piece suites. Anyway, I was hurrying along this road when I saw a light.

I stopped. It was a fire, on the low ground to my left, where the old canal ran a hundred years ago. There was a smell on the wind, a sweetish, smoky aroma that made my parched mouth water. Somewhere, down there among the debris and dying grass, somebody was cooking meat.

I left the road and moved onto the slope, silent on my canvas shoes. I went half-crouching, the pistol gripped tightly, across the slope and down. I don't know what I meant to do. Ask a silly question, perhaps. Have you see a little boy pass this way. Or maybe I hoped for a mouthful of meat. I don't know. I crept up behind a clump of withered elders and looked down into the place.

The fire was in a ring of stones. Two men sat cross-legged before it. There was one of those things over the fire, made from sticks – a spit, with a lump of meat on it.

Behind them was a shack with a sack hanging over the doorway, and beyond that stood an old, cream caravan with boarded-up windows. As I watched, the sack was pulled aside and a woman came out of the shack. She was fat, with long black hair and a man's overcoat. She came and stood by the fire. One of the men said something and she laughed.

The smell of the meat was driving me crazy. I couldn't see any weapons about, and yet I didn't show myself. In these times, a man with food was like a lioness with her cubs, he was liable to attack any intruder on sight.

As I stood, undecided, I became aware that somebody was moving on the slope above and behind me. I crouched into the black thicket and screwed my eyes into the darkness. My scalp prickled.

Two people were coming down. One carried a bundle over his shoulder. The woman by the fire heard them, and called in a harsh whisper, 'Syl? Terry?' Her companions started to their feet. One of them jerked a handgun from among his rags.

'Yeak, okay.' A woman's voice. They were close now, the

firelight glancing from hands and faces as they came down. I shrank into the shadows, biting my lip, my hand clammy on the pistol-butt. I could see them plainly, and it seemed to me they need only glance in my direction to see me. I held my breath, resolved to slip away if the newcomers passed me by.

As they came fully into the firelight, I saw what it was the man carried, and almost cried out. It was Ben. The little guy hung limp over his shoulder. The man had a hold of one leg, and the kid's head bumped against his back as he walked. I crouched, staring incredulously as he strode by. The shock must have switched my brain off. As soon as he'd passed I leapt to my feet and yelled, 'My brother! He's my brother!'

I was lucky they didn't gun me down on the spot. As it was, I'd forgotten all about the woman. Before I knew what was happening, the two guys by the fire had handguns trained on me and the woman was on the slope behind me with a club in her fist.

'Stand still!' The two men crouched, glaring at me over their weapons.

The woman behind me said, 'Your brother, is it? Well, you'd better go down then, hadn't you?' She brandished her club. I raised my hands and walked down onto level ground.

The guy with Ben had put him on the ground by the fire. The kid's face looked dead white and there was blood in his hair. The other woman, the one who'd been there all the time, knelt beside him. I looked at her. 'Is he all right? Where'd they find him?'

The club-woman prodded me in the back with her instrument. 'You keep your gob shut!' she hissed. She smelled horribly. She was upwind of me but I could smell her all right. One of the men laughed. I looked at him. His face and hands were filthy, his beard and hair matted and dusty-looking. I looked from one to another of them. Dirty faces in the firelight. Something about them. Weird, shifty eyes. I shivered.

The woman by the fire said, 'He's hurt. Bad. You better come look.' She laid a paw on his cheek, rolling his head over to one side.

My mind wasn't working. Frantic with worry, I moved

round the fire and fell to my knees by the kid's head. Too late, an alarm shrilled in my skull. The guy who'd laughed, laughed again, and the woman with the club was right behind me. I threw myself sideways, knowing it was futile. Somebody shouted and then the guns started firing.

I flung myself across Ben's body. The kneeling woman gave a sort of grunt and toppled over with blood on her face. The man who'd carried Ben crumpled forward and landed on the fire. A shower of sparks slammed out from under him and the lump of meat rolled onto the grass.

I heard another shout and twisted my head round. Rhodes was on the slope, his face shining in what was left of the firelight, hosing the camp with submachine gun-fire. There was someone else, too, shooting from a different angle. Bullets slammed and whanged all over the site, raising puffs of dirt and little spurts of shredded turf. I spread myself over Ben's motionless body and pressed us both close to the earth.

It seemed to go on forever. Every second I expected the impact of bullets tearing into me, flinging me off my brother's helpless frame. I lay with my eyes screwed tight and my teeth clenched, rigid, wondering what there could be left to shoot at. After a long time, it suddenly stopped and I was left with a ringing in my ears. I opened my eyes and sat up.

The place was a shambles of torn, bloody earth with ragdoll-figures on it. The man in the fire was starting to cook and when I caught sight of the club-woman I was sick down my clothes. The man with Rhodes was a woman. She came over, slinging her gun, and went down on one knee. She put her ear to the kid's mouth, straightened up and said, 'He's all right, I think. Best get him back to Kate, though.'

Rhodes had gone to the riddled caravan, kicked the door in and stuck his head inside. Now he crossed to the shack and kicked it over, stamping about on the remains till they were flat. A mouse couldn't have survived inside. He came and looked down at me. I knew he'd have something to say. Something sarcastic. I'd acted like a pillock and deserved it for once. I looked up from wiping puke off my jeans with grass. I'd get my bit in first.

110

'Thanks,' I said. 'You saved our lives.'

'I know.' He kicked a bright shellcase. 'And used up precious ammo in the process.' I was about to retort on the unnecessary duration of the firing when he added, 'From now on, Lodge, I suggest you stay near the house. And keep your precious brother with you, unless you want him to end like that.' He nodded towards the wrecked fire. The dead guy's clothes were smouldering.

I didn't know what he meant. 'Him?'

'No, not him,' snarled Rhodes. He moved the half-cooked lump of meat with the heel of his boot. 'This. The kid was nabbed by Purples, you great looby. Another hour or so and they'd have eaten him.'

THIRTY-TWO

'Why Purples, Mr Branwell?' He was busy. We all were, but I couldn't get it out of my mind. Of all the things I'd seen since the nukes, that was the most loathsome. I knew now why Rhodes had gone on firing long after they were all dead. He'd been trying to shoot the whole scene out of existence, like there never were any Purples.

Branwell answered me, pouring petrol into the car's tank. 'There was a song. A long time ago. A pop song. The Purple People-Eater. It was about a monster that went round eating people. It was a kids' song really but I believe it topped the charts. I suppose somebody remembered it and started calling cannibals Purples. I'd try to forget it now, if I were you; you're going to need all your mind to get through the next few hours.'

We were going. Tonight. The past twenty-four hours had been hectic, so hectic I'd scarcely had time to feel scared. We'd got Ben back to the house, fixed the bump on his head and started right in getting ready. Now most of the work was done. The time was approaching and I was frightened. I kept thinking about the Purples, but in between I thought about dying, and it had me a lot more scared than when Booth was leading me out to be shot. Crazy.

We'd all gathered in the big room at the house, and Branwell had talked to us. I kept remembering that, too. 'We have to succeed,' he'd said. 'We'll only get this one chance. If they beat us off, they'll come after us and wipe us out.' Great.

He'd sent some people up to the camp to try and organize a rising among the inmates to coincide with our assault. They were people who'd continued to live in the ruins of Skipley right through the winter. Kim's sister's husband was one of them. They'd pretend to have had enough, and give themselves up at the camp in exchange for a bunk and clean water to drink. Nobody up there would suspect anything. It happened all the time.

We'd set off up the road at one-thirty a.m. There was a truck of theirs out along the Branford road with an APC. A party of our guys would ambush these vehicles as they tried to return to Kershaw Farm. When the sentries at the road-block heard our motors, they'd think it was the truck coming back, and by the time they rumbled us we'd be on them. Car One, with the rocket-launcher, would be in front. It would fire its rocket into the roadblock, and then go through with the Land-Rover right behind, up towards the main gate. There they would park across the gateway, blocking it.

Meanwhile, Car Two and Car Three would have left the road further down, where the camp started. The inmates would have cut the wire at the bottom corner, right where Booth had led me to be shot. Car Two was to drive through the gap in the wire and race up towards the farm, using the rows of huts for cover. Car Three, with me in it as well as some others, would go round the bottom of the camp, outside the fence, and drop us off halfway up the other side. We were to go on foot the rest of the way, knock out the watch-towers at the back of the farm, and cut the wire there. The car would then crash through the gate that led from the camp to the new farmland, and join up with Car Two in its assault on the Farm.

It was Rhodes' plan. He'd had his spies out. There was a lot more to it than I've said – something about a diversionary disturbance inside the camp and a lot of men on foot with various jobs to do, but I never knew it all. I had a big wire-cutter which someone showed me how to use, and I'd have to get through a double fence with it while people shot at me. That was enough. When it was nearly time, I went and spoke to Branwell again.

'If I don't make it, will you look after Ben for me?' I knew it sounded corny, like something in a war film, but I wanted to think of him being okay if something happened. He was staying there at the house till next day, along with the sick and Kate and a few of the men.

He didn't laugh at me like he might have, he just grinned and ruffled my hair and said, 'Of course I will, lad. Don't worry about it.' He didn't say, 'Nothing's going to happen to you.' He was a very straight old guy.

Anyway, when everything was ready we sort of hung around, waiting till it was time to go. That was the worst part. I tried to talk to Kim, but she had her sister with her. Maureen. Maureen was worried about her husband Mike, who was up at the camp. Neither of them wanted to talk or anything. Kim looked strange with her face blacked up and a submachine-gun on her back, like somebody else.

Rhodes got on my nerves. He kept moving round from group to group as we stood about the factory floor, urging us in a loud whisper to remember our roles and wait for his signal. We'd been over it loads of times but he was like a cat on hot bricks.

I was sitting with my back against the wall and my head between my knees, half-asleep, when the signal came to move out. The people who were going on foot were to leave first. Kim was one of them. I sort of jerked awake and sat watching them all pile out through the door; searching for her with my eyes. In their rags and equipment and black-face they all looked the same but I spotted her. I got up and went over, shoving my way through the jostling crowd.

She was on her way out; part of the thick surge converging on the doorway, and I had to reach out and grab her arm to stop her. She turned, holding the sling of her weapon with one hand. People banged against us as soon as we stopped and I pulled her to one side, out of the crush. She glared at me from behind her paint.

'What is it, Danny? What d'you want?'

'I – I wanted to say something. Good luck or something. I mean, we don't know if we'll . . .' I broke off, aware that my voice was wavering; not knowing really why I'd pulled her from the crowd. She scowled fiercely.

'Listen: I told you. We've got to be hard, harder than them. Cavemen rule, okay?' She broke my grip and turned, back into the stream. I stood and watched her head among all the others till it disappeared. She didn't look back.

When they'd all gone, Rhodes stood by the door with a couple of his cronies, peering at his watch. We were to give them ten minutes' start, then follow with the cars. We were standing there, nervous as hell, when we heard the sound of a truck. Rhodes swore, rapped out some orders and ran out into the dark with two guys following. The rest of us moved forward but old Branwell stood in the doorway and held us back with an upraised arm. There was a shout from the yard, and a squeal of brakes, and some cheering. Branwell turned, peered out and said, 'It's the ambush party – they've brought a truck!'

It was a terrific boost to our morale. Usually, trucks were damaged or destroyed in ambushes, but these guys had captured one intact. There was some hurried adjustment of plans. The truck would go in front of Car One, so that the sentries at the barricade would be fooled into opening up for it. The car and the Land-Rover would dash through after it, and some guys in the back of the truck would deal with the sentries from behind. By the time all this had been worked out, it was time to go.

We left the factory and got into our vehicles. Car Three was packed. Besides the driver and myself, there were three men with submachine-guns and a woman with the crossbow. It was her own crossbow and she was reckoned to be an expert at it. She was to deal with the sentries in the towers behind the farm. We set off, with bits of each other's gear sticking into us; bumping along to the moor road and swinging right to begin the long climb. The armour on the windshield, and all the extra passengers put a strain on the engine and we whined and jerked our way up the steep twisting road. We showed no lights and, though all the other vehicles were in front of us somewhere, we couldn't see them.

I sat, squashed between two men, hugging my big wire-cutters and thinking about Ben. I wished for the thousandth time that things had worked out better for him; that no nukes had fallen and he was just a little lad at school, learning to read. They used to say we had nukes to protect our way of life but where was it now?

I was busy with these Spacer-like thoughts when there came a sound of shooting from somewhere up ahead and we stopped briefly. There were flashes in the sky. I could see the others' faces by their light and knew they were scared like me. It had begun, and soon now we'd be safe, or dead.

We jerked forward suddenly, swerved right and then I could see the wire of the camp on my left as we bounced over the rough ground. There was a fire somewhere inside the compound and I caught a brief glimpse of Car Two in silhouette against it with weapons bristling in the windows. Our vehicle did a screaming left-turn, flinging us all into one-another and then we were climbing; racing up the perimeter of the camp towards the farm, skidding to a halt by a wire-strung gate between towers.

'Out!' This mate of Rhodes' was with us. He more or less bundled us out onto the bumpy turf. A beam of light from one of the towers came swinging down, glancing off the car. We flung ourselves flat. One of the men fired off a burst and the light went out.

'Come on!' The man who was giving all the orders jumped up and started running up the slope. We all followed, clutching tools and weapons. Car Three roared into motion behind us, heading for the gate. We heard the impact as it rammed the wire.

After that, things followed so quickly that it's all a bit of a blur, looking back. We were shot at from the towers but there was little light and nobody got hit. When we arrived at the back of the farm there was already a lot of commotion inside the wire, with flares and gunfire and shouting. It wasn't as bad as I'd thought it would be for me; the sentries in the towers here were looking, and shooting, inwards, and I was able to get right up to the wire without drawing any fire. As I started to cut, the woman with the crossbow got busy, and the firing from the towers became sporadic. I snipped away furiously, sweating and gritting my teeth and feeling that maybe things were going our way. The purpose of the gap I was making was twofold – for our forces to retreat through if they were driven back, and for us to advance through if we were winning.

We were winning. I was through the outer fence before anybody shot at me. When they did, I never heard it above all the other racket. There was just a cluster of little impacts on the ground by my feet and a sort of pinging. Somebody yelled 'Get down!', and then I was struck a terrific blow on the forearm, as though somebody had thumped me. I lost my grip on the cutters and staggered to one side, and somebody did a rugby-tackle on me from behind. I fell down in the track between the fences, catching my cheek on a barb as I did so. The guy who'd tackled me grabbed the cutters and began snipping at the taut strands while two others shot the lights out. Something felt wet and, exploring with my fingers, I discovered to my surprise that I was bleeding. Inside the compound the racket was beginning to subside. There was a terrific bang and a blinding light, followed by submachine-gun fire and a lot of shouting.

The guy with the cutters looked round at one of the others and shouted, 'That's the rocket. They're storming the front gate!'

It was quickly over after that. Finding themselves attacked in the rear, the soldiers who'd been pressing Rhodes' men around the house threw down their arms and surrendered, so that by the time the men I'd come with went in through the gap, it was finished. I didn't see any of it myself, because I had a flesh-wound in my arm and lost some blood and passed out, and it was only when they were going round picking up the wounded that they found me and carried me into the house. It's funny how undramatic getting shot can be.

THIRTY-THREE

There were about seventy prisoners when it was over. Most of them were soldiers, though there were four policemen, six Civil Defence guys and some women and kids as well. Booth had died in the fighting. Finch was dead too; killed by a stray bullet, but most of his top-dogs had survived. There was Councillor Mrs Walker, his Food Officer. She'd been responsible for the slop doled out in Ramsden Park and had probably poisoned the Spacers. There was Lightowler, Chairman of the Hospital Management Committee before the nukes, who'd been the Health Officer, and Stroud, the Information Officer, who'd written the lying instructions about the non-existent hospital and all that. Captain Laycock, the TA officer in command of the troops was alive, and so was the MO, Lieutenant Renton.

Rhodes wanted to shoot them all, except Renton, who was a doctor. He said they didn't deserve to live, and that some of them were war criminals. Branwell argued with him, pointing out that the soldiers had had to do as they were told, and that you can't have war criminals when you're not at war. Rhodes wanted to know how he could say we weren't at war when we'd just attacked and captured their stronghold, and how had these pipsqueaks, as he called them, swung places for themselves in the deep shelter in the first place? There was this deep shelter under Kershaw Farm, which must have been built on the quiet long before. Nobody in Skipley knew it was there. Some pal of Rhodes's had found Finch hiding in it when the fighting was over, and had fired the stray bullet that ended his life.

Anyway, most people were on Branwell's side, so Rhodes had to be content for the moment. I missed all this of course, but Kim filled me in after, when she visited me in the hospital hut.

Two days later they started fetching the sick up from Branwell's place. They needed my bed, so they kicked me out with my arm in a sling. Ben had come up with the first batch. It was nice to see him again.

The place was a mess because of the fighting, and everybody was busy clearing up. The civilian prisoners were helping, but the soldiers were shut up in two of their own huts till it was decided what to do with them. I couldn't do much because of my arm, so I was given the job of keeping Ben and the other kids occupied and out from under everybody's feet. We played at football between the huts of the camp, which wasn't easy because of the slope; or tag and hide-and-seek. It was warm, and there was a feeling of optimism in the April air.

When the house and its surroundings were in order and everybody had been allocated a place to sleep, old Branwell turned his attention to our long-term future. Among the great heaps of stores and provisions we'd found about the place were a lot of seeds of various kinds – beans, potatoes, swedes, stuff like that. Branwell had been a smallholder. He knew all there was to know about growing stuff, and he started organizing us into working parties to take over the farm Finch had started. Everybody set to work with a will, because Branwell saw to it we were decently fed and there were no rifle-butts. My arm was mending, and soon I was able to dispense with the sling and take my place in the field. The kids were handed over to Kate, which suited Ben down to the ground.

We didn't take the wire down, mainly because we were all too busy, but we didn't mend it either, and nobody manned the gates. As soon as they learned of Finch's overthrow, the remaining inhabitants of the ruins started coming in. Within three weeks or so there were four hundred of us, including the prisoners, and rations became meagre. Rhodes kept on chipping away, grumbling about taking all comers, but the success of the attack, coupled with everybody's optimism now, made Branwell a popular leader and nobody took much notice of him. He never lost an opportunity to be unpleasant with me, but I didn't care. It was spring. Things were stirring in the soil and Kim, now that the immediate dangers had receded, was beginning to lose her hard shell. One day, as I was hoeing between some rows of new-sprung radish, she came over to me with a rare light in her eyes.

'Hey, Danny, guess what?'

I looked up, wiping the sweat from my forehead with the back of my hand. 'What?'

'Maureen's going to have a baby.'

'Oh. Wow.' I didn't know what to say. I mean, if I'd been a woman, living like we were living, I don't think I'd have wanted a baby. It didn't seem much of a world to bring a kid into. Kim looked highly chuffed though. She put her hands on her hips.

'Is that all you can say, Danny Lodge?'

'No. I mean, it's great, Kim. If that's what Maureen and Mike want. It's not going to be easy though, is it? Bringing a kid up in all this?'

She looked at me hard. 'No, Danny. It won't be easy. But it's what people will have to do, isn't it, if the human race isn't to die out?'

I hadn't an answer to that, and, as time went by, and it seemed everybody in the settlement was talking about nothing else, I got quite excited myself. It was all part of the feeling we had of things coming back to life; the phoenix rising from the ashes and all that.

One of the guys found this carved stone in a smashed church. A Green Man, Branwell said it was. A pagan god with trees sprouting out of its mouth and leaves all round its head: a symbol of Spring, when life comes out of death. We set it up by the farmhouse door because it seemed appropriate. That's how optimistic we were.

June came. Branwell had this calendar he made himself. It

started from the day after the battle, which he reckoned was April 15th. He didn't know for sure of course, but he said it was only days out if it was out at all. So forty-six days after we took Kershaw it was June. We'd cleared a lot of land, twenty acres according to Branwell, and it was all planted. Swedes, potatoes, beans, radish, lettuce and cabbage. We'd rounded up a few scraggy chickens, too, that scratched about in a coop in the yard. So far, they'd laid no eggs at all.

There were generators for electricity, and quite a stock of fuel to run them on. Some of the guys were looking at ways to preserve vegetables by freezing and even canning, if they could get the metal. There was some pretty good radio equipment in one of the rooms upstairs and this was manned round the clock by people who knew what they were doing. They listened out for any transmissions from elsewhere, and transmitted themselves at frequent intervals in the hope of making contact with other settlements or even the Government or something. We were always talking about the Government, and how it must have survived in its own deep shelter, but all they ever got was static.

Branwell let the soldiers out. Their CO, Laycock, gave an assurance that they'd co-operate in the running of the settlement and give no trouble. The civvy prisoners were released too, except Mrs Walker the poisoner, whom several people had sworn to get.

After the soldiers got out, some of them took to keeping watch at night. Habit, I suppose, but nobody came near. If there were Goths or Purples about they stayed well away. Rhodes got pally with the troops and would spend hours with them in their huts, laughing and playing cards.

Kate and some others organized a school for the kids. They'd been running wild long enough, and were in danger of turning into little savages. I expected protestations and tears, but as it turned out Ben seemed only too happy to go, and that went for the others, too. There were about fourteen of them altogether, aged between five and eleven. The older kids in the settlement, those over eleven or so, had long ago adopted adult roles. They'd had to. They had the rudiments of an education already, and were certainly not going to start going to school with the little ones. I asked Kate what sort of things she was going to teach.

'Reading,' she said. 'And writing.'

'What for?' I asked. 'There's nothing to read, and who are they going to write to?' She laughed and called me a pessimist. These skills have to be preserved, she said. Branwell talked to them a lot about morals, loving one another and not fighting and all that, and I could see some sense in that. They spent a lot of time outside, too, watching and helping in the field, so that when their turn came they'd know how to grow their food.

Another thing Branwell did was to set up a chapel. At least, he called it a chapel, though it was only one of the huts on the slope. New chapels are supposed to be consecrated or something but there was no clergyman in the settlement and nobody else knew how to do it. He nailed a wooden cross he'd made on the door, and said that would have to do.

He announced a thanksgiving meeting in the chapel. After all the horrible things that had happened to us, I didn't think anybody would go, but the place was packed. Ben and the other kids went with Kate, but I didn't go myself. I didn't see how things like nukes could happen if there was somebody up there looking after us.

Kim didn't go either. We'd talked about it, and she felt the same as me. It was a bright morning that promised a hot day, and we went down to the edge of the field and sat looking out over the ruins of Skipley to the bluish hills beyond. We talked, and then the singing started and we fell silent, listening, and when it stopped there were tears in Kim's eyes and I had to swallow hard a few times too. Neither of us believed, yet I think we both sensed that the chapel and the singing sort of completed our settlement, changed it from a camp to a village, like the village out of which Skipley had grown. I think we felt ourselves at the beginning of something, a new Skipley perhaps, or a new world, peopled with our children. Branwell's children, who would love and laugh and give no thought to war. I think it was something like that, and whatever it was it was beautiful. I wish we could have halted time right then, and stayed like that forever.

THIRTY-FOUR

June gave way to July. Gradually, our life settled into a routine, and a kind of healing process began inside our heads. You could feel it. Minds that had been bruised by crisis after crisis, wound up tight by constant danger, began to unwind. We hoed between the rows of as yet invisible crops whose whereabouts were marked with lengths of twine stretched on sticks. We picked stones, scattered manure from the chickens and Branwell's donkey, and scraped away irradiated topsoil to increase the acreage of our cultivated land. We talked about Maureen's baby, calling it 'Ours'. 'Our first child,' we said. 'The first of many.'

Rations were low. No more new people were coming in, and there was a slow but horribly steady toll of fresh fatalities from the ravages of radiation, but still the food we had would have to last some months yet, till the first crops came in. We were hungry most of the time but we learned not to notice it.

The huts were divided into three sorts – single women's, single men's and married quarters. Some of the kids had no parent, so they were accommodated in a hut of their own with Kate and another woman to look after them. As things began to get sorted out, quite a few couples went and got married in the little chapel. They weren't really married of course, but old Branwell said some words over them and people sang and it was the best that could be managed. One day, walking in from the field at sunset, I spoke to Kim.

'Listen, Kim. You know how I feel about you, and you said you liked me too. Why don't we get married? We could take Ben out of the kids' hut and be a sort of family. What d'you think, huh?'

She was silent for a while. We walked towards the compound with our hoes on our shoulders; bone-weary in our grubby clothes. All round us, others were walking, too, singly and in groups, talking quietly or thinking about the meal they'd soon be eating. When we passed inside the wire she turned aside and led me down behind the row of women's huts. She hooked her fingers through the wire and stood looking back towards the field. After a moment I saw that she was crying.

'Hey,' I whispered. 'What's up? What did I say?' She shook her head without looking at me. 'Nothing. I'm scared that's all.'

'Scared? What for? I didn't mean to scare you. What did I do, for Pete's sake?' She shook her head again.

'You didn't do anything. It's Maureen. The baby. I'm scared for the baby.'

I laid a grubby hand on her arm. 'Maureen'll be fine, Kim. Doctor Renton's watching her. Is there something wrong with Maureen or something?'

She pressed her forehead into the mesh. 'No. Nothing that shows.'

'Well, then!' I moved, laying my arm across her shoulders. She shook it off, twisting round to face me. Her cheeks were smudged with a mixture of tears and dust and her voice was shaky.

'Did you ever hear of Hiroshima, Danny?'

'Of course I did. Who didn't?'

'Did you read about it? About what happened to the people?'

'Yes. It was bad, Kim, really bad, but it wasn't a patch on what's happened to the whole world now. Why are we talking about Hiroshima, Kim?'

She turned back to the fence to hide her face from me. 'I'm not talking about what happened right away. I mean what happened after. I'm talking about the babies.'

'The – oh, Kim.' The babies. The babies of Hiroshima. I'd read about them all right. Babies with no legs, no arms, no stomach. Babies with two heads. Forty years after, they were still being born like that. I tried to take hold of her but she twisted away.

'No! I don't want that. It doesn't help. I want you to tell me it's not going to be like that with Maureen's baby. I want you to say it's going to be all right. The first of many. That's what I want, Danny.'

I stood with my arms dangling, looking at her. I didn't know what to say. I didn't know why it hadn't occurred to me; the possibility that the kid might be born deformed or something because of the radiation Maureen had taken in. Maybe it had occurred to me, only I'd buried it, refused to think about it. Kim regarded me accusingly over her shoulder.

'Well? Can you do that, Danny? Can you say it's going to be all right?'

'Can you tell me why you haven't been thinking about it all these weeks as I have? Why you're pestering me to marry you so we can make a monster too?'

I looked at the ground. I didn't have an answer that made any sense. 'I've been thinking about it,' I said. 'Only I've kept it underneath, y'know? We have to hope, Kim. There were normal babies in Hiroshima too.'

'Not many.' She turned away and her voice was flat. 'Not even with the best medical attention in the world. And like you said, that was nothing, one tiny bomb. So you go on hoping if you can, only don't expect me to push it to the back of my mind and rush off and marry you and live happily ever after.'

I don't know what I'd have said to that, if Ben hadn't come running to say why weren't we getting washed ready for dinner. He stared at Kim like kids do when they see a grown-up cry. I put my hand on the back of his shaggy head and steered him back the way he'd come. He kept trying to look back. 'What's up with her?' he demanded.

I shook my head. 'Nothing, Ben. She's a bit fed up, that's all.'

He was silent for a moment, then he said, 'D'you think she'd like to see this? Tim and me found it under the school.' He fished in his pocket and pulled out a crumpled fistful of rag. I kept walking and he opened it up, trotting at my side, and held it out towards me. 'Look.'

I looked. In his dirty palm, half-moribund, a butterfly lay. At first I took it for two butterflies but then I looked again, cried out with revulsion and knocked it from his hand. It spiralled to the ground, fluttering ineffectually its seven misshapen wings.

THIRTY-FIVE

In August it was hot. The bombs had done something to the atmosphere, so that the sun came up in a sort of fiery haze and burned behind it all day like a big fuzzy ball. It messed up the radio too. The soldiers listening out were half-deafened all the time by fantastic crackling noises. Not that there was anything else to hear. They'd swept the wavebands, tuning in on every possible frequency, and there was nobody there. The feeling grew that we were alone in the world.

There were no birds. It was a long time before I noticed this and when I did, I couldn't remember whether I'd seen any since the nukes. Maybe they'd all been wiped out the day it happened, or perhaps they'd just gradually faded away. Anyway, there were none now.

Another thing. You know how in August you could look across a valley and all the other side was greens, different greens, with a square of yellow here and there where corn grew, or oilseed rape? Maybe you don't know. Maybe it never came back. Well, that had gone too. Looking across the valley where Skipley lay, it was like looking at some place in North Africa or somewhere. All reds and browns and yellows, and clumps of black where dead trees were. I suppose that ought to have warned us, but it didn't. We were all so busy looking after our first crop, we didn't notice that nothing much was growing any more.

We got these terrific electrical storms, and the rain made our seeds germinate so that the dark, wet soil was crossed with rows of fresh green shoots. We took away the twine and worked like mad, wielding our hoes to chop down the weeds that came thrusting up between the rows. The little stone effigy by the farmhouse door had got into our heads and we were blinded by our own optimism. The Green Man. Life out of death. Where there's food there's hope.

As the little plants grew bigger it became apparent even to us that they weren't the proper shape. Most of us were town people, but even a townsman knows what the top of a turnip looks like. These were coming up sort of clumpy and not opening out like they should. We had canes with strings for the beans to climb, but they didn't. They rose about four inches and fell over to twist slowly along the ground like sick brown worms. There should have been flowers on them, but none appeared.

We carried on desperately, telling ourselves it was just the tops. Underneath, the turnips and swedes and potatoes would be fine. No beans maybe, and no cabbages, but plenty of potatoes. In Ireland, they used to live on potatoes.

Then one morning, when we'd been at work maybe an hour, Branwell came out with Rhodes and Captain Laycock and Doctor Renton. They went slowly up and down· the rows, plucking the leaves and rolling them between their fingers, all the time conversing in low tones. Everybody pretended to be working hard, but all eyes were on the three men as they made their grim inspection. Perhaps we clung to some forlorn hope that things were not as bad as they appeared. If so, it was quickly dashed. Branwell stooped, grabbed a handful of leaves and uprooted a swede.

It wasn't a swede at all. On the end of the stalks dangled a grey, shapeless lump about the size of a cricket ball. The old man flung it from him with a muffled exclamation and pulled another, holding it up so that the others could see the mass of warty pulp.

They began pulling up potato plants and turnips, too. Everything was the same. The turnips were smaller than the

129

swedes, and just as ugly. The potato plants had nothing on them at all, only a tangled mass of sick roots with clumps of clay stuck to them. Finally Branwell straightened up and looked at us all. We'd abandoned the pretence of working and stood, leaning on our hoes while the hearts sank within us. It was a big field, and he had to shout to make us all hear.

'I'm sorry,' he said, 'but as you can see, our vegetables are not developing properly. Mr Rhodes and myself have suspected as much for several days, and I believe most of you have too. It may be that we didn't remove the top soil thoroughly enough, or perhaps the plants were affected by radiation which fell with the rain. In either case, there's no point I'm afraid in going on wasting our time and energy on them. I would ask you not to be too despondent, however. We have food enough for several months if we are careful, and Mr Rhodes has some ideas about re-supplying the settlement in preparation for winter.' He broke off, spoke briefly to his three companions, and then added, 'If you will return to your quarters now, we will meet together in about an hour to discuss the situation. Thank you.'

We trooped back to the compound. Hardly anybody spoke. We threw down our useless implements in a pile by the gate and fanned out, each heading for his own hut. The kids came out of school with their teacher, to find out why we were back so soon. Somebody told Kate, and she told the kids it was nothing and ushered them back inside. Ben looked back at me as he went, and I could tell he knew it was something bad.

We packed the chapel for the meeting, and a lot of us had to listen from outside. Few of us had any suggestions as to how we might cope with the new situation. Branwell said the rations would have to be reduced still further, except for the sick. When he said except for the sick, he got a sharp look from Rhodes which he didn't see. Rhodes' idea was the sort of thing you'd expect. He proposed forming raiding parties, to go out and look for supplies, 'wherever they may be found.' He meant, even if we had to kill people to get them. I could see from Branwell's face that he was heartbroken, but then we all were. Rhodes told us he'd be asking for volunteers starting tomorrow, and Doctor Renton chipped in to say he thought the raiding parties were a good idea anyway, because we were getting low on medical supplies and you can't grow those in a field. If it was an attempt at humour it fell flat.

We dispersed. Most of us went and lay down on our beds. We'd known really I suppose, but now that it was official, the weight of it bore down on us and filled us with despair. After all the horrors of the past year, things had seemed to be improving at last. Now, it looked as though we were pretty nearly back to square one. We'd have to start going out again, scratting among the desolation for something to eat. Looking over our shoulders for Goths and Purples. Wandering into areas of high radiation without knowing it.

We moped, warded off the kids' questions when school finished for the day, and straggled up to the refectory for our frugal meal. It was a glum affair. I'd just sat down with Ben when Kim came in, looking wild. She looked about till she spotted me and started towards my table with something in her hand. As she made her way along the narrow, crowded aisles I saw that she carried a misshapen swede. She stopped at the end of the table and leaned across, dangling the thing in front of my face. Her eyes burned with a febrile light.

'See this, Danny Lodge?' The hand that held it quivered. The whole room had stopped eating and was looking at her. 'D'you know what this is, eh? Well I'll tell you. It's a Swede, but it's not your ordinary, everyday swede. Oh, no. This is a Hiroshima swede, Danny-boy, and we also do Hiroshima turnips, Hiroshima beans, Hiroshima spuds and Hiroshima rotten cabbage. Oh yes, and I nearly forgot. Hiroshima babies. We can do you a nice Hiroshima baby if you like.' She stepped back, flashed a look about the room and screamed, 'The first of many!' Then she flung the swede from her, turned, and ran weeping from the room.

THIRTY-SIX

I found her down at the bottom of the compound, where the wire had been cut the night we took the farm. Branwell had put up a bit of a shed there for the donkey and I knew she liked to visit the animal now and then.

It was dusk. The inside of the shed was very dim. It smelt sweetly of clean hay. She was sitting on an upturned pail, with an arm draped over the donkey's shoulder and her head resting against its flank. The donkey, its halter twisted round a post, stood with its head down, patiently chewing. I paused in the doorway, unsure of my welcome and reluctant to intrude. I must have made a sound of some sort though, because she turned her head quite suddenly and saw me.

'How long have you been there?' Her voice was wavery, as though she'd been crying for a long time. As I moved forward I saw that the donkey's coat was wet where she'd rested her cheek.

'I just came. I've been looking everywhere for you. Are you all right now?'

She turned away. 'Yes. I think so,' she said, huskily. 'I'm sorry I shouted at you. I don't know why I did it. I'll never be able to go in that refectory again and I don't know how I'll face the others in the hut tonight. They were all there.'

'It was nothing,' I said. 'They'll understand. It probably hadn't occurred to them. Like me. They'll understand now.' I wanted to comfort her. She looked so young, so slight and thin, in her grubby jeans and torn check shirt. She should have been worrying about discos and boyfriends and O-levels, not fallout and deformed babies. She was stroking her cheek up and down the donkey's flank.

'D'you think so? D'you think they will understand? I wish they would, because you don't know what it's like, Danny. There's twenty-nine of 'em in my hut. Twenty-nine, and all they ever say to me is you are looking after that sister of yours, aren't you? We can't have anything happening to her and the baby now, can we? What do you hope it'll be, a boy or a girl? And all the time I'm trying to forget about the rotten baby so I can get some sleep at night. Last time somebody asked me that last one I said, yes, I hope it's a boy or a girl, but they didn't get it, they still kept on.'

I knelt in the hay beside the pail and reached out my hand and began stroking her hair. She kept her face on the donkey's flank and didn't pull away.

'I know it's easy for me to say,' I told her. 'But you've got to stop worrying all the time. You'll drive yourself barmy, and there's nothing you can do about it. You know it's all decided now, one way or the other. We've just got to hope, Kim. It's all we can do.'

'I know. I know there's nothing anybody can do. That's the awful part of it. Waiting. I've been doing nothing else for weeks and I'm tired and scared and fed up. Oh, Danny!' She turned and flung her arms round my neck and buried her wet face in my shoulder. 'What's going to happen to us all? How's it going to end. Danny?'

'Not with a bang but a whimper.' She was tiny in my arms, sharp-boned and quivering, like a little bird.

'What?' She lifted her head a little so that I felt her breath on my ear.

'It's a quotation. Forget it.'

'Oh. Yes, I've heard it before. Don't say that.'

'Sorry. Branwell did the same thing to me, ages ago. We were looking at Mum's grave.'

'What did he do?'

'Quoted something at me. He who places his brother in the land is everywhere.'

'What does that mean?'

I shrugged against the weight of her arms. 'It means, all over the world men are burying their brothers. Ever since he said it, I've watched Ben like a hawk. Y'know, looking for signs of a dose and that. So you see I do know what it's like, worrying.'

'Yes. I'm sorry. When you're really worried about something, you tend to think you're the only one. I feel better now, Danny. Better than for ages.'

'D'you think you ought to see Doctor Renton? See if he's got something that'll make you sleep?' I don't know why I said that. I felt tender and weak and hot and excited, all at the same time.

She squeezed my neck. 'No. Not now. Let's just stay here for a while like this, and then I'll be all right. I do want to be your girl, y'know.'

'I'm glad.'

How long we might have stayed there if we'd been left undisturbed, I don't know. I sort of half-lifted her down into the hay beside me and, as we kissed, pushed gently till she was lying with my arm under her neck and both hers round mine. We were kissing, long and hard, when suddenly she twisted her head away and hissed, 'Ssssh! Listen!'

I didn't want to listen. I followed her mouth, trying to cover it with mine. She let go my neck and pushed me away. 'No. Listen.'

I sat up, frowning with irritation. Kim was sitting too, with her head on one side. I listened. It was a motor, a long way off. Coming up the road from Skipley perhaps.

'It's a motor. So what?' I was anxious to recapture the mood of a moment ago. I felt it slipping away.

Kim looked at me, big-eyed in the gloom. 'Do we have any motors out?'

I shrugged. 'I don't know. Why?'

She began to get up, brushing hay from her seat. 'Because if we haven't, it's somebody elses, isn't it? It sounds – different somehow. Listen.'

I stood up and listened, facing the doorway which was covered with a curtain of sacking. The thrumming was closer now. Much closer, and behind it I fancied I could hear a swishing noise, like when someone whirls something round and round their head on a rope. My heart kicked against my chest and I stood a moment with my mouth open, unable to speak. The noise swelled, till it seemed the thing was right outside.

The sacking rippled and blew inwards and somebody shouted on the compound. Kim stared at me, incredulity stamped on her face.

'It's a –'

'Helicopter!' I ran to the doorway, tore aside the curtain and we tumbled through, gazing up.

It hung snarling, black against the twilit sky, turning slowly on its axis as though someone inside was taking a careful look at us. People poured from their huts, shouting and waving their arms, their faces turned up in the downdraught that stung their eyes and whipped their unkempt hair.

The machine completed three slow rotations through three hundred and sixty degrees then flew, nose-down, away over the wire in the direction of Skipley. Cries of dismay followed its departure, and everybody ran to the gateway and milled about on the slope, waving, watching the winking green navigation-light dwindle against the hills across the valley. When we could see it no longer we broke up into chattering, gesticulating groups, or wandered away in a daze by ourselves, unable to believe what we had seen.

It's not possible to describe adequately what the arrival of that helicopter did to us. It was a sort of instant dislocation – the end of life as we'd come to expect it would be, a glimpse of a world we thought had gone forever. We surged about, all talking at once, so that the air was thick with a thousand speculations. It was a British helicopter, sent at long last by the Government to rescue us. It was Russian, and tomorrow enemy soldiers would come and occupy the farm. One wag said it was the Barratt helicopter, come to survey the land for a housing-estate. Finally, after I don't know how long, Branwell managed to get us quiet enough to announce a meeting in the refectory and we trooped up there, laughing and talking. I went up with Ben riding on my shoulders and my arm round Kim's waist and tears of – I don't know – happiness or relief, pouring down my cheeks. I didn't care. I wasn't the only one.

Rhodes had had his field-glasses on the aircraft, and it was Swiss. As soon as Branwell announced this, everybody started telling everybody that it was obvious; the Swiss had deep shelters, enough for everybody, in the mountainsides. They'd survived, and now they were here to save us, to shower us with condensed milk and chocolate and cuckoo-clocks. Any rescuer would have been rapturously welcomed, even a so-called enemy, but the fact that we'd been found by the Swiss was the icing on the cake, the little barrel of brandy round the St Bernard's neck.

I've forgotten what else was said at that meeting. Something about awaiting rescue calmly and meeting it in a dignified manner. We sat deaf and bubbling, like kids on the last day of term, and when old Branwell finally let us go we cheered him with tears in our eyes and sang, 'For He's a Jolly Good Fellow', and ran outside to turn cartwheels and practise our yodelling. It was a long celebration, a short sleep, and a rude awakening.

THIRTY-SEVEN

They came mid-morning, grinding up the road in a jeep and a truck while a helicopter, a big one, hovered above our heads with guns sticking out of it.

We'd all come out to greet our rescuers, all except the sick. We stood close together just outside the wire. Most of us weren't feeling too good. We'd broken out the remaining rations the night before and stuffed ourselves, and we weren't used to it. We'd spent a short, uncomfortable night, unable to sleep for excitement and indigestion, and now, as we watched the soldiers jump down from the truck, we were troubled by the vague feeling that all was not quite as it ought to have been. There was a ragged cheer, but not the sort of rapturous greeting we'd imagined ourselves giving.

The soldiers formed a semicircle and moved forward slowly, their weapons pointed at us. I suppose we'd had visions of smiling guys in leather shorts and braces. When they were about ten yards from us they stopped. Nobody was smiling. One of them stepped forward. He had what looked like Captain's pips on his epaulette. He had a pistol in a holster too. He said, 'Who is in charge here?'

Branwell moved out from among us. 'I am, I suppose. Allow me to say on behalf of us all that you are a most welcome sight.'

The officer inclined his head slightly but did not smile. 'Thank you. You are the Commissioner?' Branwell shook his head. 'No. I am – adviser, I suppose, to these people. There is no Commissioner here.'

'Oh?' The officer arched his eyebrows. Is this not Sub-regional H.Q.? Sub-region Two-point-one?'

'It was,' replied Branwell. 'We were forced to take it over.'

'Why?'

Branwell shrugged. 'It's a long story, Captain. Shall we talk about it in the house. We can manage a little coffee, I think.'

'Certainly not!' The Captain's tone was frigid. 'I see an officer in uniform. There – behind you.' He pointed. 'Who are you, sir? Why do you not speak for these people?'

Captain Laycock stepped forward. His uniform was in tatters and his hair curled about his ears. Beside his Swiss counterpart he resembled an scarecrow.

'I was Senior Military Officer here, Captain. My name is Laycock.'

The Swiss officer stared at Captain Laycock coldly. 'Why are you not Senior Military Officer here now, Captain? Were you . . . relieved of your command?' Captain Laycock shook his head.

'No, Captain, I was not. My men and I were compelled to surrender to these people. They were armed then, and they came under cover of darkness. The Commissioner had – exceeded his authority, sir.'

'Indeed?' The officer's face wore a sarcastic expression that reminded me of Rhodes. 'You surrendered, and yet you do not look to me like a prisoner of war. Your men mingle with the crowd quite freely it seems. I think that you have co-operated with your conquerors, Captain.'

Laycock inclined his head. 'That is true, Captain. We have all of us had to work together in order to survive.'

'I see,' said the Captain. 'Then this establishment is what we might call a commune?'

Laycock nodded. 'Yes: I suppose it is.'

'Commune, as in Communist?'

'No! I mean, damn it all. You're twisting my words.'

'No I am not. You have seen fit to run this Headquarters

along communist lines, rather than in the manner laid down by your Government.'

'No. I've already explained. It was necessary –'

'It was your duty to protect your Commissioner, Captain. And if you became a prisoner of war it was your duty to escape. How many of you are there here?'

'What?'

The Captain flipped a hand in our direction. 'Is this everybody, or are there others?'

'There are others,' said Laycock. 'The sick. When the British Government knows the circumstances, I'm sure it will exonerate everybody here at once.'

The Captain laughed, a brief, harsh sound. 'There is no British Government. We must make a count.'

'What?'

'A count. The numbers here. And don't keep saying what.'

He turned and barked something at his men. Four soldiers slung their weapons and ran to him. He spoke briefly, gesticulating towards us and the camp. Two men went towards the gates. The other two started shoving us about, counting. Branwell went over to the captain.

'Will you please tell us what's happening?' he said. 'Are we to wait here, or do we go with you?'

The Swiss regarded the old man coldly. 'You remain here, naturally. What do you think I am going to do with a crowd of broken-down Englishmen? March them to Berne?'

Branwell ignored the sarcasm. 'Will we be given food and medicine?'

'Perhaps,' the Swiss replied. 'In due course. And in the meantime I must complete my count and report to my superiors, so please get out of my way.' He brushed the old man aside and strode up towards the camp. The two soldiers had finished counting us. They fell in behind him.

Branwell stood, gazing after them with hurt in his eyes, and a soldier came and prodded him back into line. The helicopter had landed somewhere inside the wire. We stood there, staring dumbly down the muzzles of their guns, while the captain and his men went through all our stuff. He counted the sick, prodded about among the stores and made a pile of our weapons, all the time making notes in a little pad. He'd taken Laycock along to show him where things were and he told us about it afterwards.

It took about two hours. The kids got restless. Some of them wanted to go to the toilet but when Branwell asked the soldiers they ignored him. Maybe they didn't understand English. Anyway, by the time the captain came back there were some wet pants and a lot of helpless anger. As soon as he came striding through the gateway, Branwell called out, 'Captain, we are British Citizens and you are treating us like criminals. Do you intend to help us, or not?'

There was a bang and a roar. Somewhere behind us the helicopter was starting up. The captain had to shout his reply.

'The term British Citizen has no meaning now,' he yelled. 'There are groups like this one all over Europe. You must wait your turn!' The helicopter rose from beyond a line of huts and he had to grab at his cap to keep it from being blown off. He turned and started down towards the jeep. The soldiers followed, walking backwards at first, covering us with their weapons. The helicopter thrashed about over our heads till the Swiss were in the vehicles, then it swung away down the slope and out across the valley. The jeep bounced off down the road and the truck followed. We all stood and watched them go, and when we finally traipsed back into camp, we found they'd immobilised the vehicles and taken our weapons away.

THIRTY-EIGHT

Branwell called us together in the chapel. He looked tired and sad and somehow smaller than before.

'There is no food,' he said, 'Because like a fool I let us eat it all last night. There are no weapons either. Mr Rhodes and some of his men and women have offered to go out and find both. They will have to go on foot, because the Swiss took the rotor-arms out of our vehicles. They do not know how far they might have to travel, nor how they will protect themselves along the way. Nevertheless they are prepared to go, and I must let them try because it is our only chance.

'While they are gone, those of us who remain must hang on as best we can. We have clean water. We must forage for food and fashion makeshift weapons. We must give priority to feeding the children, and the sick. It may be that the Swiss will return soon, but if not we must work together, so that when Mr Rhodes and his party return, we can start all over again.'

Kim hissed something I didn't catch.

'What?'

'I said, they won't come back, will they?'

I glanced at her. 'Who? The Swiss?'

She made an impatient sound. 'No. Rhodes and that lot. Why should they?'

I couldn't answer straight away. Her words had brought an icy pain to my guts, because suddenly I saw that she was right.

When I got control of my vocal chords I said, 'You're right. Why should they? They don't go in for this lame-duck stuff, looking after kids and invalids and that. I'm going to say something!'

'No!' Her fingers gripped my elbow and she glanced about her. 'Let them go. I might be wrong, and anyway we can't stop them. If they've decided to go they'll go, and they'd probably kill anyone who got in the way.'

She was right, of course. They left – Rhodes, the pick of his guerilla band and some of the soldiers, and they never came back. The rest of us hung on, scratting for edible roots, burying our dead, growing thinner. The weeks went by. The weather became colder and Branwell tried to hold us together. He really tried. 'They'll come,' he kept saying. 'They had a long way to go, on foot, but they'll be back, you'll see.'

The roots we gnawed on were probably contaminated. They were certainly hard and bitter. Our gums bled and there were griping pains in our stomachs. School stopped. The kids wandered about, clutching their guts and whining. I found myself watching Ben all the time, his blown-out belly and matchstick legs. Maureen lay moaning in her hut. Mike sat all day beside the bed with his hands dangling between his knees, staring at the floor. Kim spent a lot of time there too. Renton looked in from time to time and mumbled something, but he had only words left to treat people with.

I suppose it was a couple of months before Branwell finally gave up on Rhodes. He got us in the chapel and told us, and everybody could see he was ill. There were only about a hundred of us left, and we fitted into the place easily. The old man said Rhodes and his party must have met with an accident, but you could tell he didn't believe it. He urged us to hang on and wait for the Swiss, but his heart wasn't in it.

A thin wind whipped flurries of early snow across the compound. People started to slip away. I suppose they thought they'd have more chance in twos and threes, fewer mouths to feed, more territory to forage on. Those of us who stayed, stayed through fear, or because of old Branwell. Kim stayed because of Maureen and I couldn't leave Kim.

The baby came one December afternoon. It had no mouth, and it died almost as soon as it was born. Renton hurried straight from Maureen's bedside to Branwell's. The old man died that night. I went to the stable to tell his donkey, and because I knew Kim would be there.

The donkey stood, a worn grey bagful of bones, chewing away at nothing while Kim wet its flank with her tears. I sat down well away from them. I didn't speak, but I think the donkey knew. I sat there with my back against the wall, listening.

At first I didn't know what I was listening for. Then I realized I was hoping the helicopter would come, like the last time we were here. I made a small, involuntary sound and Kim turned her head.

'Danny?' Her voice was a fragile thing.

'Yes. You all right love?' Stupid, meaningless question. She turned away, resting her forehead on the donkey's flank.

'We're leaving, Kim. Ben and me.'

'Yes.'

'I expect you'll stay. With Maureen.'

'I don't know. It doesn't really matter where we are, does it? We'll all die in the end, wherever we are.'

'Everybody dies in the end.'

'You know what I mean.'

I ran my fingers through my hair. It was stiff, matted. We'd all stopped caring for ourselves weeks ago. The phrase pre-Neanderthal passed through my mind, followed by an overwhelming feeling of sadness. After a while I said, 'There's a place I know. Holy Island. There's a causeway to it that's cut off when the tide's in, and a castle. It's a long way from anywhere else. We might be all right there.'

'We might,' she said wearily. 'But I doubt it. And anyway it's hundreds of miles away.'

I shrugged in the dark. 'If Ben could make it, you could.'

She sniffed. 'How d'you know Ben could make it, though?'

'I don't, but I'm not staying here. Not now.'

'It's winter, Danny. You'll . . .'

'Die? Better to die doing something than to sit here waiting for it. Will you come with us, Kim?'

'I – I don't know. I don't know if I can go on any more, Danny. I don't know if I even want to.'

I didn't say anything for a while. Kim stroked the donkey's knobbly spine and I sat watching her, remembering something Branwell had said a long time ago. They haven't killed that, have they, with their bombs and their hunger and their cold. They haven't killed that.

He'd meant love: my love for Kim, and he'd been right. They hadn't killed it. They couldn't. I got up and went over to her.

'Kim,' I said. 'I love you. You know that, and old Branwell knew it too.' I told her what he'd said, that day when Dad died and I'd felt like dying too. I told her I'd probably have given up long ago if it hadn't been for her. 'I can't stay here,' I cried, 'But I won't go without you. Come with me, Kim. Let me try to make a place for us, somewhere.'

She was silent for a while, and then she nodded. 'All right, Danny,' she whispered. 'We'll give it one more try for Ben and the old man.'

We slipped away that night, Ben, Kim and me. Ben rode, clinging half-awake to the bundle of spare clothes on the donkey's back. We left without saying goodbye, because you can't just say goodbye. You've got to say other things too, and there was nothing else to say. Morning found us in the rolling hills, going north.

THIRTY-NINE

'Why not try one of our chip-butties?' said the fading sign in the café window. My guts yearned. We'd been five days on the road and this was Osmotherly. There was no damage here, no bomb damage, I mean. People had been through looting, because all the doors were kicked in and most of the windows smashed, but nobody would waste a bomb on Osmotherly.

I looked across the donkey's neck at Kim. 'Why don't we try one of their chip-butties?' I said.

'Shut up, Danny.' Her feet hurt and it was cold as hell and coming on to sleet.

Ben, perched on the animal's back, said. 'Can't we stay here, Danny? I'm tired and my feet have gone funny.' I laughed. 'Your feet have gone funny? What about mine and Kim's? We've been walking all day.'

It was probably about three in the afternoon. We'd spent the previous night in a farm building and had found a pile of rock-hard swedes in a corner. We'd gnawed some for breakfast. They were like doorknobs. The donkey had polished off about twenty of the things and its sides had blown out like a flaming balloon. It was the first decent meal the poor creature had had in months. I grinned up at Ben.

'Aye, I reckon we can spend the night, kiddo. Doesn't look like anyone's around.' We'd come halfway down the main street by now, Kim and me gripping our cudgels, peering in doorways and down alleys. Nothing stirred, not even a cat. I could have fancied a nice bit of cat. I nodded towards a house with windows still intact.

'We'll kip down in there. Hang on a minute.' I left them standing in the middle of the road and approached the house, my club at the ready. No smell of occupation reached my nostrils, only the damp, flat odour of decay. I did a quick tour of the rooms. There was a beat-up suite, a rusting gas-cooker and some junk on the floors, broken cups and that. Two upstairs rooms had beds, but looters had taken the mattresses and bedding. I called Kim across.

'Unload the donkey,' I said. 'And get Ben bedded down. I'm off back to that café to see if there's any grub.' I started back along the empty street, head down against the sleet.

It had been a pretty rudimentary café, a hikers' place with a juke-box and cheap plastic furniture. The juke-box stood rusting in a corner and somebody had smashed all the furniture. The display counter was glassless, the tea and coffee machines ripped out. I hadn't expected to find anything here; it was the cellar that interested me. I found the steps, pulled a torch from my pocket and went down.

It was single cellar, whitewashed, with tiers of shelving round the walls. I flashed the torch about. The shelves were bare, except that on the top one, in a corner, stood the gas-meter I'd been looking for. I went over, reached up and thrust my hand behind it. As I had hoped, there was something in the cobwebbed space between the meter and the wall. On tiptoe, I pulled out two rusty tins and a damp, disintegrating packet. If you pile stock on a shelf near a meter, something is bound to fall down behind it now and then. It was always happening at home.

The packet had contained breakfast cereal, but now held only a lump of mould. I dropped it on the floor and examined the tins by torchlight. The labels were damp and spotted with black, but enough of the print remained for me to see that one held soup and the other spaghetti. I grinned, and was heading for the steps when I heard something. I stopped, dead.

It was a familiar sound, a sound I'd once thrilled to and never thought to hear again, the snarl of high-powered motor-bikes.

There were several of them. I couldn't tell how many, but they were approaching at speed. The roar of their engines swelled till I fancied I felt the vibration. I doused the torch and stood, gazing at the ceiling.

The din reached a crescendo and began to recede. I sucked in some air. Whoever they were, they'd gone straight through. I moved, and as I moved the fading note changed. There was a coughing, a series of rapid detonations and some revving. The bikes were coming back, moving slowly. They'd seen something.

I thrust the tins in my pockets, grabbed my club and was halfway up the steps when a pair of legs in black leather appeared at the top.

'Stop there!' I stopped, feeling myself go cold. The legs were not familiar, but the voice was. It was Rhodes.

A second man appeared with a torch, which he shone in my face. I jerked my head aside, screwing up my eyes, and Rhodes said, 'Well, well, well, if it isn't young Lodge. What're you doing roaming about the countryside, eh? When I saw that mangy animal up there I thought it was old Branwell, come to show me the error of my ways. Now there's a sanctimonious old wassock for you!'

'You shut up about him!' If he hadn't had a gun I'd have gone for him. I was scared, but I was blazing mad as well. 'You're not fit to say his name. Why the heck did I have to run into you, of all people?' I knew I'd had it, I suppose. I only hoped he'd think I was alone.

He smirked. 'It goes to prove the old saying, doesn't it, Lodge: all roams lead to Rhodes.' He laughed loudly, nudging the man with the torch.

I stood, forcing myself to gaze levelly into the glare, hoping Kim and Ben would get away. Rhodes' laughter stopped, like somebody had switched it off.

'All right Lodge,' he snarled. 'So maybe it wasn't the world's funniest gag. You should've made the most of it anyway, because it's the last you'll ever hear. Drop that club and start backing down. Slowly.'

I'd forgotten I held the club. I opened my fingers and it went clattering down the steps. I didn't care, as long as Kim got away with the kid. You're not hungry when you're dead, and you don't feel the cold. I backed down, as slowly as I could. Every second was precious. Rhodes and the other guy started down, keeping the same gap between us.

'Right.' I'd reached the damp flags. 'Over against the wall. Turn your pockets out.' He'd seen the bulges. I pulled out the tins and my torch, and his mate came and took them from me. I leant my back against the wall. A few flakes of whitewash fluttered down and settled on my jacket. My hair brushed the underside of a shelf. I felt tired.

'Goodbye then, Lodge.' I closed my eyes.

The submachine-gun made a terrific racket in the confined space. They say you don't hear the one that gets you, but I wouldn't know about that. All I know is, there was this hellish clatter and I sort of stiffened and nothing hit me and I opened my eyes and Kim was on the steps with a gun, and Rhodes and his pal were lying in these very relaxed postures on the floor.

Before I had a chance to say anything, a motor-bike started up outside. There were a couple of shots, and the sound of the bike departing. Kim let out an oath and started up the stairs. I grabbed the tins and Rhodes' gun and followed her.

I found her, fists on hips, glaring down the road. Two bikes stood nearby, glugging petrol onto the ground. The donkey was cropping grass some yards away, oblivious to the driven sleet.

'What happened?' I said. Kim gave up gazing after the vanished machine and kicked one of those that remained. 'I heard 'em coming,' she said. 'I was just getting Ben wrapped up. I ran outside and they were coming back towards the café, three of them. They'd seen the donkey, I suppose. I forgot to tie him up and he'd followed you. I saw two of 'em go in. They left the other one watching the bikes. They hadn't seen me. I got my club, sneaked up and belted him over the head. I thought I'd killed him. I took his gun. He must have come round, heard the firing and scarpered, after shooting holes in these things so we couldn't follow. I should have hit him harder.'

'Why?' I wasn't thinking straight. 'What's it matter, Kim? He's gone.'

'Yeah, but he'll be back. There were twenty-five in Rhodes' party, and I bet they've all got bikes. We've got to get out of here, Danny. Now!'

There's a sort of instinct for self-preservation that goes on operating long after you've stopped caring. As I followed Kim back towards the house, a part of me was wishing she'd left me to die and when, a few moments later, I shook that poor kid awake and saw the handfuls of his hair on the blanket, I knew that half of my reason for living was dying.

AFTER

We left the village and walked uphill, avoiding the road. Presently, around dawn, Kim saw a house. It was hidden from Osmotherly by a fold in the hills. She made sure it was empty and we moved in.

That was more than two years ago. Ben died of a creeping dose just a few days after we settled in, and we buried him in the garden. It was raining, I remember. We'd wrapped him in sacking but there wasn't quite enough and we could see a bit of his bald head glistening. I know you're supposed to say something over a grave but I didn't know what, so I said what Branwell once said. I said, 'He who places his brother in the land is everywhere.' Just that. It's hard to talk when you're crying.

There was this book in the house. A ledger with nothing in it. What I did was I started to write down everything that happened after the nukes. I thought that someday, a long time from now, somebody might read how it was and maybe it would stop them doing it again. When spring came and we moved on I was going to leave it under the floor but Kim said, 'Don't, Danny. It's not finished.' She meant our story. 'Write *to be continued*, and bring it along.'

So I did, and she was right. It *wasn't* finished. There was this to add.

We reached Holy Island in May after the longest, hungriest, most frightening journey two people ever endured. At first we travelled by day, taking turns riding the donkey, but after twice narrowly escaping capture by bands of purples who seemed scarcely human, we took to lying up in barns or woods during daylight hours and travelling at night. We daren't light fires for fear of attracting attention, so what little food we scavenged was eaten raw. We ate frogs, slugs and woodlice. Often we'd throw up immediately afterwards, but it was good protein when we managed to keep it down. We chewed fresh young nettles that stung our mouths, as well as dandelion roots and anything else we thought might be edible. And yes, in the end we were driven to slaughter and eat the donkey.

We had the biker's gun, and we did it with that. I mean, Kim did. I couldn't do it, but I was glad enough of the raw meat. I know it seems cruel, but neither of us would have lived to reach Holy Island without it.

We arrived in May, very early in the morning with sunrise gilding the sea. The tide was out, and we might have set off across the causeway at once if we hadn't noticed a smudge of smoke over the silhouette of the castle. We installed ourselves in the rusted shell of a van and watched the causeway all day. When the tide returned to cover it we hadn't seen anybody, but the smoke was still rising. We waited, weak with hunger and fatigue, taking turns at dozing. It was twilight when the waters withdrew once more from the causeway. We were discussing whether to emerge and take a chance when we saw movement. A vehicle detached itself from the island and began crossing the causeway in a haze of spray. Kim and I watched its approach. There was nothing to indicate a connection with our presence till, on reaching the slipway, the vehicle swung right and came straight towards our hiding place. Too late to withdraw, we could only keep our heads down and hope we wouldn't be seen.

It was a forlorn hope. The vehicle, an APC complete with armament, halted ten metres away, its machine gun trained on the van. The hatch was raised. A man appeared with a loudhailer.

'*Attention, occupants of abandoned vehicle. You have been under observation for some time. You are completely surrounded and heavily outnumbered. Throw out the automatic weapon and any other arms you possess. Do this now.*'

Kim gazed at me in the thickening gloom. 'A Rhodes soundalike,' she croaked.

I nodded. ''Fraid so. Do we fight or give in?'

She sighed, shaking her head. 'You heard him, Danny. Surrounded and outnumbered. Maybe they'll give us one good feed before they shoot us.'

She threw out the gun. There was a pause, then the loudhailer quacked again. '*Step out slowly, one at a time, with your hands on your heads. Any sudden movement will result in immediate death. Do this now.*'

Kim crept out, then me. We stood shivering on the tarmac in a stiff sea breeze, hands on heads. It seemed a long way to have come, just for this. We honestly thought it was the end.

But it wasn't. Instead it was a beginning. Over the next few hours – hours during which we ate, drank, bathed and were given clean clothes – we learned that the place we'd come to had three names: Lindisfarne, Holy Island and New Beginning. The first two were old names, the third quite recent. New Beginning was an agricultural commune like Branwell's MASADA, but with one crucial difference: it was guarded day and night by men and women with an armed forces background and all the equipment they were likely to need. A sort of kibbutz, in fact.

So here we are. Kim and I have been here two years. We're expecting a baby soon, and we're not worried. It will be New Beginning's fourth baby, and the other three are thriving. No missing bits, no extra bits, if you know what I mean. If it's a girl it'll be Kate, after a nurse we once knew, and if it's a boy it'll be named for little Ben, my brother. In the land.

READ MORE IN PUFFIN

For children of all ages, Puffin represents quality and variety – the very best in publishing today around the world.

For complete information about books available from Puffin – and Penguin – and how to order them, contact us at the appropriate address below. Please note that for copyright reasons the selection of books varies from country to country.

On the worldwide web: www.puffin.co.uk

In the United Kingdom: Please write to *Dept. EP, Penguin Books Ltd, Bath Road, Harmondsworth, West Drayton, Middlesex UB7 0DA*

In the United States: Please write to *Consumer Sales, Penguin USA, P.O. Box 999, Dept. 17109, Bergenfield, New Jersey 07621-0120*. VISA and MasterCard holders call 1-800-253-6476 to order Penguin titles

In Canada: Please write to *Penguin Books Canada Ltd, 10 Alcorn Avenue, Suite 300, Toronto, Ontario M4V 3B2*

In Australia: Please write to *Penguin Books Australia Ltd, P.O. Box 257, Ringwood, Victoria 3134*

In New Zealand: Please write to *Penguin Books (NZ) Ltd, Private Bag 102902, North Shore Mail Centre, Auckland 10*

In India: Please write to *Penguin Books India Pvt Ltd, 706 Eros Apartments, 56 Nehru Place, New Delhi 110 019*

In the Netherlands: Please write to *Penguin Books Netherlands bv, Postbus 3507, NL-1001 AH Amsterdam*

In Germany: Please write to *Penguin Books Deutschland GmbH, Metzlerstrasse 26, 60594 Frankfurt am Main*

In Spain: Please write to *Penguin Books S. A., Bravo Murillo 19, 1° B, 28015 Madrid*

In Italy: Please write to *Penguin Italia s.r.l., Via Felice Casati 20, I–20124 Milano*

In France: Please write to *Penguin France S. A., 17 rue Lejeune, F–31000 Toulouse*

In Japan: Please write to *Penguin Books Japan, Ishikiribashi Building, 2–5–4, Suido, Bunkyo-ku, Tokyo 112*

In South Africa: Please write to *Longman Penguin Southern Africa (Pty) Ltd, Private Bag X08, Bertsham 2013*